The Willow Tree

Komal Akhtar

All rights reserved.

Copyright @ 2024

No part of this publication may be copied, reproduced in any format, by any means, electronic or otherwise, without prior consent from the copyright owner and publisher of this book.

ISBN: 9798339878063

Imprint: Independently published

Cover Design by: Evgeniia Gurcheva

To my mother, who will never be able to read her daughter's words or hear her voice. Just know, you are everything to me.

To my father, who has the purest of hearts. I am by all means an extension of your goodness.

To my husband, my lifetime companion and my best friend. I love you.

And most importantly, I thank Allah. My success is only by him.

To every woman out there.

You are worth it.

Naghaar

Talia

I'm sat under our willow tree, writing this letter to you as if you could read it. I tell myself that if we focused on the things that united us, the world wouldn't be as fractured as it is... I told myself that...a million times... Yet this made no difference to us. I lived in suffering yet still somehow felt alive and I lived in a cage, but you managed to set me free even though this world clipped your wings. But I'm still holding onto the hope that I see you again.

Soon.

Letter 396

Yours, Talia

The town that I lived in was called Naghaar. It was situated at the foot of the Himalayan mountains and sat boastful and alone on the plains of Asia. During its' summers flowers of all shapes and colours competed to kiss the skyline and their fragrance created a beautiful concoction of serenity for the senses. The Ondas River ran directly through the town, supplying it with fresh mountain water and seafood of the highest minerals. In the far-off distance the Indian desert loomed and reminded residents of its' golden grainy blanket. Golden meadows and flourishing vegetation wrapped around the town like a radiant sheath of natural beauty Every now and then sand from the desert would travel in synchronisation with the wind, its' gentle ballet performance would float across the land and sprinkle grains on the lands of Naghaar.

As a child, I would run barefoot through these meadows with the sun casting my shadow onto slippery brooks and valleys. My imagination would ignite at the sight of the colossal tree trunks and in that short time I would feel the purpose of living. But that free childhood had become a longing memory, one that I would often revisit when I drifted into a deep slumber. One little accident turned those moments into distant fleeting memories. It was a time when the clouds had welcomed me with the first burst of rain that year. I was around ten years old. I could feel the rainfall sink in between the strands of my black hair and touch my scalp delicately. It was the kind of rain that was warm when it touched the skin and sweet when it hit the lips. I had been running in the field and the mud had begun to soften and sink between the gaps in my toes. I could remember how it felt.

As I ran faster, I embraced every raindrop that hit my paper like complexion. The bright colours of the meadow would then transform in front of my very eyes, and I was suddenly transported to the depths of the forest, listening to the branches crack beneath my feet and hearing the leaves whisper to one another. Suddenly, my foot lost contact with the ground and I slipped down a steep muddy hill, tumbling and falling, watching the world spiral around me as if I was being mixed and swirled into liquid. I hit my head on a rock but luckily the impact of the fall was cushioned by the soil on the ground. As I lay on my back, I watched as the crimson liquid that seeped out from the gash in my head polluted the ground. I could see the sky swirling and swaying in rhythm with my pounding heartbeat. The heat and pain seeped across my temple and sparked my lungs to scream out in pain. I didn't remember much else, but I remembered a blurry figure stand over my trembling frame. And then I blacked out.

The Naghaari council had sent out search parties and my mother wept for hours and hours at the possibility that she lost her one and only daughter. By 4am, through the dark veil of the night, a Naghaari man had found me sat upright against a tree trunk. There was thick blanket over my body and a white torniquet wrapped around the wound on my head. In the freezing night-time temperature, he carried me home to my mother and by morning the whole neighbourhood had swarmed around my bed with handpicked flowers from the meadow and baskets of herbed bread. To my mother's relief, I had recovered fairly quickly, and the local doctor had confirmed that there was no sign of long-term damage.

That night voices trickled in through the gaps in my bedroom floorboard and I gingerly made my way down the stairs to listen in. I sat on the stairs, peeked through the wooden bannisters and watched as men dressed in blue robes and tall black hats sat in the living room.

"You are lucky she survived" said one of the men.

"She could've been killed".

My mother, Samara sat with her arms crossed, glaring at

the men with a frightened expression. I had never seen my mum look so pale.

Another man spoke. "Something needs to be done. Those Pariah's are roaming the forest after midnight. Before we know it, they will invade, kill us all and breed with Naghaari men" he retorted.

"Has she said anything?" the first man asked.

My mum shook her head.

"She was found with a blanket and bandage. Those Pariah's are manipulative. Trying to weasel their way back into our society with their perceived good will. I propose a law where the Pariah's have a curfew they must abide by. This way they can stay out of the darkness and thus reducing the risk they pose for us. Only then will Naghaar stay safe".

"I agree" another man spoke with a deep tone. "It is about time we set some boundaries".

Around a week after that incident, my mother had warned me not to play in the meadow again. I cried and screamed but my mother was adamant on her word. The following week the topic of the Pariah girls became part of our daily learning and the world as we know had changed drastically.

The story of the Pariah girls began back before any of us could remember. It was said that at the time Naghaar was hit with the worst drought anyone had ever known. That summer, the sun had travelled to its highest point and scorched the surface so much that heat pirouetted off it. The neighbouring dry sands of the desert filled pockets in bricked walls and fruit in carts had cracked and shrivelled under the blazing heat. An abundance of sand deposited onto Naghaar's land and areas that were once cobblestones had been covered with dry hot sand. This created a small desert pan between both sides of town.

The main side of town was where many of the Naghaari's lived. Here all the markets, the school and council chamber were located. The other side of town was mainly used to breed cattle, and often farmers would usually work on that side, bucking wheat or collecting sheep dung to be used to create the base for cooking fires. One early morning that June, the Ondas River stopped flowing through the town and ceased the abundance of water and food that residents so often were taking for granted. It was decided by the council that rationing needed to be introduced until fruits turned ripe and water flowed again.

During this time, Naghaar experienced its' first baby boom. Almost every baby born that year was a girl. This eruption of the female population had come at the worst of times. The extreme heat and lack of food and water meant that women would camp for days outside the council chamber in the hope that the council would see the gravity of the situation. Mothers cried as their breastmilk dried, and children struggled to play under a scorching temperature that lasted for 4 long years. But the Naghaari council were reclined in their palaces of greed.

The council, who decided the laws and made decisions for the Naghaari people, consisted of the male heads of 18 families. They were corrupt, driven mad by their power, and had been rumoured to be rolling in the money that the rich families of Naghaar had paid. The rich of the town would pay a small percentage to the council and in return they were given a supply of food and water every month. When this news was made public, animosity grew but nothing could be done.

The birth of all these babies added to Naghaar's troubles. Because to them these girls were more 'costly' than boys. Clothing, sanitary cloths, medical care and marriage were all contributors to that 'cost' and many families had resented their daughters for it. As for the other side of town, the cattle had died, leaving a barren empty land. The meat of those dead animals was rationed out, but the supply lasted only a few short weeks. The farmers and men of the poorer families had left town for days on end because of the loss of farming jobs, and they went to work on distant farms and factories in order to put food on the table. With the lack of sons in families, these men began to struggle knowing they did not have many male predecessors to help them in the future.

There came a point when families of low income could no longer afford to raise their children on their daily wages, and this is where the story of the Shandaars and the Roons began.
The Shandaar family were approached by the Roon family. The Roons were known to be rich and affluent. They had grown into their money through property investments but everyone in Naghaar knew that Mr and Mrs Roon struggled to conceive. Despite all their wealth, money was not enough to buy the blessing that was parenthood. Until one

day they heard that Mrs Shandaar had given birth to triplets. In an already overcrowded home, Mrs Shandaar had expressed to the whole neighbourhood that she didn't know how she would accommodate three more children, especially three more daughters. She muttered and complained to every passer-by and eventually this news reached Mrs Roon. Mrs Roon approached her during the Thursday market rush hour and tapped her on her shoulder.

"Mrs Shandaar?".

"Yes?". A plump woman turned to look at Mrs Roon. Her eyes looked drained, most likely from a lack of sleep. Her skin sagged in several places and her wrinkles spread from her heavy eyebags to the edge of her receding hairline.

"Mrs Roon! It's an honour!" she smiled shaking Mrs Roon's hands warmly. "How can I help you?".

"I heard that you are struggling with your newborns…" Mrs Roon replied.

"Yes, you heard right" she sighed. "I have too many kids

and now I've just had 3 girls! Imagine the cost!".

Mrs Roon looked solemnly at her. "You are very lucky, how I wish to be a mother".

"Lucky?!" Mrs Shandaar shrieked. "Ufff…I would love for someone to take them off my hands. It damn near killed me giving birth to them".

Mrs Roon felt a burning anger inside of her. How selfish of her when other women such as herself would die to take her place. Mrs Roon thought to herself how much she desired to be in her position. And then an idea came to her. It was a bold one for sure but after 18 years of infertility, she was willing to try anything.

"If you had a chance to, would you give your children away to someone who wanted them?" asked Mrs Roon. And after a quick five-minute discussion, Mrs Shandaar had agreed to give Mrs Roon her triplets for the price of 500 garoles each. Mrs Shandaar had become richer in a mere couple of minutes and danced around at the prospect that she would have less children to go home to. Mrs Roon cried tears of happiness because she finally had become a mother not to one but to three beautiful girls.

But this innocent exchange triggered what we now called the allotment system.

Once news spread of Mrs Roon's and Mrs Shandaar's trade, poor families rushed to the gates of the wealthy with their daughters in their arms. This reaction triggered the council to meet up late at night.

"So, we have had pressure to allow the children of families to be traded. Poor families cannot afford to pay for their children in this drought. The prices are too high for them to afford".

"What do the rich gain?" an elderly grey bearded man said.

"What do you mean?" asked another man.

"This law cannot be passed if there is no benefit for the

rich. They need to gain something from this. *We* need to gain something from this".

The council deliberated late into the night and by 5 in the morning, the grand leader Laris Roman had passed the allotment law. The law stated that poor families were allowed to trade their children on 2 conditions.

1. that the child or children must be of good health before the exchange

2. the child must be married off by the age of 16 to the man who offers the highest bid. This was to be known as the seeking ceremony. However, on the condition that girls were not healthy enough to be exchanged or refused to marry, they must be sent to the pariah zone.

The Pariah zone was created on the empty bit of land, right opposite the town where the farms used to be. A large fence was built using timber and wood. Across the top of the fence was sharp barbed wire, and the land of the zone merged into the forest behind. The perimeter was built by the council and the rich had donated money to fortify it.

These conditions were signed by the families and deals could then be made at any agreed price. As the months and years went by, baby girls of the families were given away and girls were married off as soon as they turned 16. You must wonder what benefit the rich got from this? It was simple. The girls exchanged into the rich families were raised in exceptional health. They received the best education and the best medical care. Because of this, it was easy to distinguish between girls that belonged to the rich and girls that belonged to the poor.

So, what happened to the girls that were not exchanged and did not want to be kept by the poor? She was a drifter. A nobody. Hanging between the classes, simply existing until the council decided that she needed to be sent to the pariah zone.

The seeking ceremony took place once a year. Girls would be taken to the council chamber in the centre of town and from there, men of any age could offer up any amount of money to marry the girl. If the rich family of the girl were happy with the price, bidding would stop and without delay the girl would be declared 'sought out'. The marriage then usually took place as soon as possible.

Many fathers were stubborn and would not accept offers under a certain threshold. These men found it difficult to sell their daughters and eventually conformed and lowered their prices. The rich got even richer, the poor gave up the blessing of parenthood in order to ease their own burdens and the girls were the ones to suffer.

In the centre of town, the council chamber had built a large wall in dedication to the allotment system, this became known as the carved wall. Every year, girls who were exchanged between families successfully had their names etched into the walls with sharp knives. I had seen my name on it when I was eleven. And although part of me didn't understand it then, by the time I was 14 I understood that I was given away by my birth family because I was a burden on them, and that very soon I would be married off to a man my parents would choose. Although I had never known my birth parents and perhaps never would, I wanted the chance to tell them one day that I was worth keeping. The drought had to everyone's relief finally ended yet the system became so engrained in the town that families continued to exchange their children. It was a disease that possessed even the sanest minds. But, over time this system that shed so much importance on creating and moulding 'perfect' girls began to change for the worst. When I was younger, the story of Amara spread like wildfire. She was sought successfully at a high price, but her parents had not told her future husband that Amara had a debilitating bone disease. Her husband found out a few years later when Amara collapsed and after being taken to a hospital the doctor broke the news. That same night, Amara's husband demanded the council to change the law. A 3rd condition was added to the allotment system:

3. if the adoptive parents or husband no longer wanted to keep the girl, the following reasons must be applicable: She has been involved in inappropriate premarital activities She has a physical or mental impairment She has been uncompliant to her husband or adoptive parents' wishes

From then on, girls who were unsuccessfully sought out had become the targets of the third condition. Girls who were unhealthy, girls who were unable to procreate, and girls who were disobedient were all sent to the Pariah zone within the space of a few days. The worst part of it all, was the way they were sent to the zone. Once a decision was made against her, she would be pinned down, any time or place the man decided, whether that be in the middle of the night or whilst she was out buying groceries and she would be branded. This was a ritual of searing the woman's forehead with a hot iron rod, recently scorched in an open fire, and burning her skin with the sign:

~~PA~~

The official mark of a Pariah girl.

She would then be forcefully removed from town and taken to the zone, where she could either turn and walk into the sector or attempt to re-enter Naghaar by running across the desert pan and in the process get shot down. Many women had been killed trying to sneak back into Naghaar a few days or weeks later. Their branded foreheads were hard to miss. The men that took on these roles were called handlers. The so-called protectors of Naghaar. They always had their faces covered when they performed their duties and wrapped around their right arms would be a red fabric with the word *soten* stitched on to it. Soten meant saviours. Only handlers were permitted to carry weapons and they were the ones seen to be roaming the streets and forests at night, looking for any Pariah's who were out of their zone.

That was the beginning of the war between the Pariah's and the Naghaari's.

Laris Roman the head of the Naghaar council had passed away a few years ago due to old age, and the leadership was passed down to his close friend and confidant, Makni Armis. After a two week long funeral, the brutal nature of the allotment system continued to grow in popularity. It was the Naghaari's way of respecting Laris Roman's legacy.

Many families were pleased with this law, because in their minds, this ensured their adopted girls would remain compliant. Forever.

Overtime the Pariah girls became a cursed label for women who refused to conform to the ideals expected of them. These women, although strictly confined to the zone at night, were free to roam Naghaar during the day. This was so that Makni Armis could ensure the Pariah's would always be watched during the day and that they could also be put to work. During the day they could be seen cleaning toilets, picking up litter and burying bodies. Naghaari's never interacted with them apart from when they spat at them, swore at them and beat them up for simply looking at them.

No Pariah was allowed to stay in Naghaar after nightfall, and once they had done their jobs, they would return to their zones across the desert pan with the little money they made, which was around 2 garoles. That was enough to buy an apple.

As for the zone itself, it could be seen at a distant from Naghaar. There was nothing there that sustained the Pariah's. The mud was their surface, the sky was their roof, and the forest and silver fences were their walls. The terrible conditions meant that many of the Pariah's had gaunt bodies from starvation, many of them wore tattered, dirty clothes that draped over their muddy bodies. Many were young in age but had been visibly dishevelled by their filthy conditions that they looked accelerated in age.

My best friend Lucia told me of a time, a Pariah offered her a paper bird. She was very young when it happened. She told me how the woman had limped towards her groggily like she had walked endlessly for days. Underneath her thick black hair, her raven-coloured eyes were so deeply intense that Lucia said she could feel her glaring into her very soul. But she smiled slightly, and it somehow softened the wrinkles around her eyes. Lucia had taken that bird from her, but before the woman had parted her peeling lips to speak, the sound of approaching handlers made her snarl and run for cover like prey being hunted by its tracker. Some of the Pariah's couldn't physically work because of their physical ailments and there were rumours that they survived by selling themselves to married Naghaari men who weren't satisfied enough by their wives. According to these rumours, men would travel across the desert pan late at night and would emerge the next morning with leaves in their hair and their shirts untucked. The men in the Naghaar council were not excluded from these rumours either.

However, it started becoming a problem when Naghaari's began to go into the forest to hunt wild animals more often. It seemed that during this time, the Pariahs began to become more savage and started to create makeshift weapons. Until one day, 2 handlers were found dead in the forest. Since then, casualties from both sides began to emerge and the war that had only begun to simmer began to slowly worsen. Every so often, both Naghaari's and Pariah's would fight and kill one another, and one day the fighting had amounted to 45 deaths in the space of just a few days. But, somehow, miraculously, the fighting slowed down and the Pariah's and Naghaari's kept their distance from one another. It seemed as if the Pariah's had learnt to be submissive and slowly the number of killings reduced. That's not to say there were no more deaths, in fact, they still fought, but most of this was done in the darkness, in silence, and it had become so common that nobody reacted to it anymore.

Everyone had been told of the lives of the Pariah girls and every Naghaari girl had been trained to believe that the Pariah's were barbarians. And so naturally I was afraid of the Pariah's too, a deep fear that was stemmed from all the stories I got told. Naghaari nursey rhymes would teach girls the danger of disobeying the men in their families. Books would mention the life that Pariah girls lived. The fear of the Pariah girls and the danger they posed turned into words and whispers in the street. It turned to recitation, and this recitation became unequivocable terror for every young girl. No one wanted to become like them, so every girl complied in every way possible.

That was how Naghaar was ran. That was how the council kept their control.

My Bloodline

Kalei

I inhaled a large gulp of air to sustain my sinking heart. I weaved through the narrow streets. The florist's shop had bloomed, and I could no longer see the brown rusty borders of its doors and windows. Clusters of weeds sprouted out from the holes in walls and wrapped around the building like ivy. The strong smell of meat drifted down the street, I glanced over as the butcher lifted his cleaver high and brought it down into huge joints of meat. As I turned around the bend, the street had widened, and several huge houses came into view. A woman ran up to me, she shoved a bunch of white flowers in my hand and began to weep.

"I'm sorry for your loss. How is your mother?"

"She's okay" I mumbled.

"It's a shame isn't it?" she shook her head slowly, "a widow now…when is the funeral?"

"Tomorrow, at 2pm" I replied bluntly.

The woman nodded and then ran off down the street and disappeared out of sight. I looked down at the flowers, white roses that looked freshly picked. I took a moment to recollect my thoughts and closed my eyes for a brief second so I could separate myself from the clutches of my burdened breaths.

My father had died a few days ago, of a suspected heart attack whilst he was away on business. Although he was only in Naghaar a few weeks in a year, everyone knew him for the work he did to install water pipes and wells in our town. Before he had died, he had been working on trying to improve sanitation in the town, but he never made it to that meeting. He had died, alone in his hotel room, and for what? My father worked a job that took him a thousand miles away from his family and because of the distance, I very rarely saw him.

On the days he used to come home, we would sit as a family, but I always found it uncomfortable. I never really knew what fathers and sons talked about and those days passed in complete silence. But my mother loved him unconditionally. On the day he died, she received a letter early morning that informed her of the dreadful news. I was in my room when I heard her wails cut through the stone walls of the house. I found her tucked away in the corner of her room like a lost child. I had never seen my mother that way. The last four days were agonising. I called the local doctor to examine my mother because she had stopped eating and drinking. The doctor concluded she was suffering from a 'deranged loss of perception', in other words, he called her mad. He had advised me to send her to Naghaar asylum and that the council would pay for the private treatment, but I kicked him out of the house in unfathomable anger, screaming at him that she was my mother and not an animal.

Instead, I attempted to feed her and sat with her for hours until she finally had one bite from my hands. I talked to her about my day, and though she would not reply or even look into my eyes when I spoke, I felt like she could still hear me. I had received endless letters from Naghaari council members, offering their support, and they even paid for my father's funeral as I wouldn't be getting my allowance until I turned eighteen, which was still a few months away. Neighbours offered me their condolences and all the letters I received, I responded to them as best I could. After filtering through what seemed like a never-ending pile, I finally was left with a pile that had been sent from Naghaar asylum. To my anger, the council had contacted them on my behalf. I ripped them into pieces the moment I read them and scattered them on the street for the wind to take with it.

But now my father's funeral was tomorrow, and although everything, from the flowers to the coffin, to the service was all arranged, my mother didn't want anything to do with it. Perhaps it was intractable grief or perhaps it was the fact that she would have her baby any day now, and that the father of that baby would soon be in the ground.

You must be wondering why the council paid for my father's funeral and why they were so keen on getting my mother 'help'. It was because Laris Roman was my grandfather. Because of the blood connection, it was expected of me to pledge my allegiance to the council and to become a council member when I turned eighteen. And so, everyone saw me as the great heir that would continue Naghaar's legacy, and that was why I was so important. I had no relationship with my grandfather because he was so often holed up at the chamber rather than choosing to spend his time in the house. Very soon the house we lived in became a hostel for him. From the stories that used to circulate around town, Laris Roman was known to have been a strict, stubborn and incredibly obese man that towards the end of his life, he had a special chair made for him just so that people could carry him through the town. It took at least eight men of the largest build to do so.

But the truth was, I wanted to explore the world, my best friend Sami and I always talked about it. But I had only a few months left before I had to succumb to those expectations. To live up to the family name. My mother never mentioned it, she very rarely brought it up in conversations, but I could see that she wanted to beg me to accept the pledge because it would give me the best life. I would live in splendour; I could do as I pleased and have enough money that I would be swimming in it. Even one day, if lived long enough, I could change laws, perhaps even the allotment system, although the idea of that was harbouring on impossible. I had never admitted, and probably never would but I found the allotment system barbaric. If I ever expressed such an opinion, I would be most likely be imprisoned for simply voicing an opinion that went against all the council stood for. And trust me, the men that did try to protect their daughters, wives, sisters barely survived in prison for longer than a few months. But most of all, I resented the system because of the life it gave my little sister.

My little sister Meira was fourteen years of age but in those fourteen years she lived in darkness, having never once left the house. In fact, she was so elusive, that not a single person in Naghaar knew of her existence, to them only my parents and I made up the Roman family. The reality of it was that Meira was no ordinary looking girl.

When she was born, her lips looked misshaped and uneven, and her top lip was unilateral and arched high so that her small gums and tiny tongue could be seen. Meira struggled to latch on to drink my mother's milk and within a few days the slit in her top lip had begun to grow until it opened even wider, and it started affecting Meira's drinking capability. Because of this, my mum began giving Meira ordinary cow milk and Meira had been ill so often with an upset stomach because of it. A few days after Meira's birth, my mother came downstairs for the first time and rushed to draw the curtains shut so that not a single speck of light would enter the house. She strictly warned me not to let

Meira out of the house, not even in the garden in the fear that if Meira was to be seen by anyone else, they would take her away. To Naghaar, she was an unhealthy girl. She would be branded if she was ever seen. To them, she was useless.

I had become overly protective of Meira. My perspective of the world had changed once she was born. Meira had recently begun to resent me for taking away her freedom. She struggled to understand the implications of her being seen, she didn't understand that if they saw her, she would be branded and sent to the zone. I wished she could see that every single speck of goodness that would become of me, would be because her. I wished she could understand that every time she opened her eyes into mine, I saw all her laughter, her happiness and her tears and that would be up to me to guard. I would have to make sure that her life with me would be worth her reminiscing about when she was one day old and grey. But she stopped letting me in. She couldn't see it.

In a way, I didn't blame her. She had no experience of what friendship was; she never saw sunlight and she would spend her days reading books or drawing so often she began to start drawing on the walls and living in the world she built in her head. Every time someone visited our home, Meira hid in the compartment that was above the bathroom. Sometimes for hours on end she would stay there, in the dark, and wait and wait for the house to empty before she could emerge again.

"Take these please."

I had returned home after clearing my mind and I gave the flowers to the maid. I took off my shoes and made my way upstairs.

"Mum?" I called out. I gently opened the door and found her sat up in bed with a photo in her hand. "Mum?" I repeated.

I sat down beside her and gently put my arm around her shoulders. Judging by the redness around her eyes, she had been crying. I watched as she took a deep breath and then for the first time in days, she looked me in the eyes.

"I miss him" she said in an almost whisper.

"I know…" I nodded as I took her hand into mine. She looked down at the photo, it was the photo from their wedding day. She took her hand and stroked it over dad's face and in that one slow motion I could see all her thoughts. She missed him so deeply that she couldn't fathom it. She couldn't accept that the man she loved was no longer around. Although he was away so often, she would write to him every couple of days. For her, this was the longest time that had passed where his voice and hers didn't intersect across the ink on letters.

"I'm sorry…" she whispered again. "I'm such a bad mother…"

"No" I squeezed her hand tighter. "Why would you say that?".

Her voice began to break, and her lips quivered as she spoke.

"I'm such a bad mother. I haven't hugged you for so many days nor asked you how you have been. I've been so consumed in my own grief I forgot that you are suffering too".

"No mum". I placed my hand on her cheek and turned her face towards me. "Look at me". She gazed up at me with deep sorrowful eyes. "If my mother needs me, I will be there for her. Right now, I don't care about myself. I just need you to return to me whenever you are ready".

She nodded gently.

"The funeral preparations are all done. I don't want you to do anything, leave it to me okay? Just put your feet up".

"You'll be a big brother soon…" she half smiled ignoring

the topic of the funeral. She placed her hand on her belly and paused for a long moment. But that glimpse of a smile disappeared almost instantly, and she began to cry into my shoulder. She wondered how she would raise a child after so many years and she questioned how she would be as a mother again without a father present. I wanted to tell her that she had been in fact doing that for so many years, but I thought it was best to keep quiet. I did nothing but let her keep her head close to me and let her tears speak the words her tongue struggled to form.

"How's Meira?" she asked sniffling and wiping her nose.

"She's okay" I assured her. "Don't worry".

And you see, that's why I had stepped out of the house that day. I needed the fresh air. I needed to remove myself from those four walls that had started to feel like a cage. I didn't regret looking after her nor did I hate that every hour was spent in that house, I just needed some space to remind myself that there was a world outside and that one day I would eventually return to living in it.

Why couldn't things be the way they used to?

Kalei

Meira and I always had a tight bond, but the older we got, the more self-conscious she became and the more distant the space between us grew. I remembered the times I used to bathe her, play with her and put her to sleep. She would hold me tight, often begging me to stay with her through the night. And so, not being able to resist her exquisite smile, I slipped myself into bed next to her, wrapped my arms around her little torso and stroked her hair till she fell asleep. Meira was always a deep sleeper, and very often she would start snoring loudly within a few minutes. On the days I did lay with her, I never managed to fall asleep.

Instead, I would spend the hours of the night staring at the ceiling imagining different worlds or using those moments to trace the patterns on her skin.

I wanted to protect her. I wanted to be the one she could go to anytime she felt even an ounce of sadness. I wanted so much for her in a world that would give nothing back to her.

By the age of eleven, she began to grow rapidly in height, her short black hair began to grow in thin spaghetti like strips and by the age of thirteen they had reached the top of her bellybutton. Over the years, I noticed she began to watch herself in the mirror more often, she was more interested in her appearance, and sometimes she would steal mum's clothes or accessories and use them on herself. Just a few months before she turned fourteen, she begun to express feelings of self-hatred for the first time, remarking to me that she felt ugly and hated how she looked. Around the same time, she began to habitually ask me why she still wasn't allowed out, that she was old enough and that she wanted to make friends. Although I tried so hard to convince her that I would be her best friend, I suppose the idea of her big brother being her only friend didn't excite her one bit.

During the evenings, I used my spare time to teach her to read and write, and reading had become a consolation for her. In those books, she discovered new ideas, she discovered how a girl should live and I suppose that's where the animosity began to grow. What's marriage? Why am I not free? These were the kinds of questions she would ask me, and I struggled to answer all of them. I was able to tell her what love and marriage was. I was able to tell her about the allotment system and how our world was not like the world in those books, but that didn't mean she accepted it.

Not long after was the very first time she said to me that

she hated her life and that she blamed me for it. And now at fourteen, she barely looked me in the eyes, barely stayed in the same room as me. The day she turned fourteen, mum had baked her a beautiful cake made of strawberries and cream. Meira pushed the cake off the table and screamed that her life wasn't worth celebrating. Even though mum knew her behaviour had changed, it was the first time that she saw it with her own eyes. I had to watch and witness how my beautiful little sister cut every single strand that once attached me to her, to a point that I became a detached piece of fabric on her once stitched and completed canvas.

Talia

It was the day of the funeral of Mr Roman, a well-known man in Naghaar. I had never met him personally, but I knew of him. He was a rich businessman. Mother told me he was the man behind the wells we had and the waterpipes that ran through the town. That morning, I watched as my mother and father dressed up in their best attire.

My mother was a tall lean woman with square slouched shoulders and bony hands. Her hair was thin, always held up in the same tiny bun wrapped securely at the top of her head. She had never gone to school, nor did she know how to read or write. The only thing she knew was this system. To her, it held everything together. Growing up she would often tell me how important it was for me to take the herbal concoctions she grinded down for me; she mentioned how important it was for me to maintain my skin and hair and how important it was for me to obey my future husband. She drilled those expectations into me and whilst she worked hard to mould me into the 'perfect' girl, I worked hard to feel her love.

My mother was an only child, she never told me much about her upbringing, in fact she never told me much at all.

I guess it explained why she had never really understood why I was so upset the day my older brother Sarin decided to elope with his lover and leave Naghaar. He never wrote to us, and I suppose his absence only made my parents' marriage worse, but to be honest, their marriage had never been loving.

My dad Nico had been a council member for more than eight years. He had gained an undisputedly high reputation amongst our family and friends. He was short and round, with ashy grey hair and thick square glasses that always sat on the very tip of his broad nose. My father had always been extremely strict with me, and over time my mother mirrored his parenting style.
Because of father's status, he projected his expectations on me too, but his expectations weren't like my mother's. He would berate me constantly and say how I was representing

the Arman family. That if I was to do anything a woman wasn't meant to do, I would be tarnishing his name, and for that he would never forgive me. I worked hard to gain his appreciation, I desired for my father to say just once that I was beautiful or that he was proud of me. But even though he had the title of a father, a supposed guardian, a supposed protector, he only had a cold heart that was welded behind an iron casing. Over time, I told myself to let go of my expectations of him, but I could never truly achieve that. I always needed him, but he just needed me to keep my invisible price tag immaculate.

I lived in a large, stoned house with its own coal fireplace and marbled bath. We only had one maid, Gracie, who looked after the home. With only my mother and I mostly at home, Gracie, at a ripe old age of 70 found it easy to manage the home. I did often wonder why she didn't retire;

she was an incredibly old woman with one foot already in her grave. I told her often that I saw her as a mother figure, after all she had served my parents for the last 40 years, and even though she never had children of her own, I felt as if I belonged to her.

My parents often argued, especially late after midnight, about things I never really understood but it was perhaps the only exhilaration my mother ever got. Aside from those explosive arguments, my mother would sit in the kitchen with Gracie, knit jumpers (very poorly) or sit in the garden for emotional respite. Recently however, my mother had begun to scold and complain that I would fail to be sought out at a decent price when I turned sixteen. Which was only a few months away.

She would say my raven black hair was witch like, that the lack of colour in the strands of my hair resembled the lack of colour in my soul. That my pale skin was lifeless, and to reverse such paleness I would benefit from staying indoors for hours a day in the hope I would be gifted a miracle hue of redness in my cheeks. That theory never made sense to me. She would say my brown eyes had no depth and that I would be lucky if my future husband found some beauty in them. Every part of my body she scrutinised; it became so ritual like that the last few months I had begun to believe it. Unfortunately.

Every time I looked at the stillness of the water in the deep stone wells, I would see my reflection and I would notice not only every flaw that my mother so horribly dissected, but every other flaw that I had never noticed before. Until now.

My skin was not as smooth as it could've been, perhaps the dullness under my eyes made me look older in age and maybe my pink lips were too much like the salmon in the Ondas River, one shade and no depth. And now I held onto those thoughts so often, that they began to seep into me and become a defect in my already tainted character. I was my own worst enemy and I knew that. But my mind didn't allow such realisation to be at the forefront of my thoughts, so my damaged self-worth became my best friend.

However, the main thought, the thought that infected my dreams and clinched onto my nightmares was that I was going to be part of the seeking ceremony soon. I didn't know how to feel about it. My mother was too excited at the prospect of giving me away to a stranger and even though my father never brought it up, I knew on the nights he did eventually come home he searched my face for any signs of damage that may risk lowering the price of his porcelain daughter.

"Hurry up Nico!" yelled mother from the living room.

"We're going to be late!". Dad bolted down the stairs, as fast as his plump body could take him, wearing his council attire with a look of unblemished pride. The council members all wore the same long blue robes made from silk which touched their ankles. Their tall black hats were square and solid in shape. I was wearing a white dress, no other colour existed on the fabric, but it was soft to the touch and had some delicate thread work on the neckline that faintly sparkled in the sunlight. I left my hair undone, its soft waves grazed my hips, and it was brought together with a small white hair band that kept the shorter front strands of my hair tucked neatly behind my ear.

We arrived at the Patlin, the building where the funerals of the wealthy and prestigious took place. This building wasn't particularly large, its' dome shaped roof and intricate woodwork however made it an appealing place for wealthy families to say their goodbyes to their loved ones. The seats were wooden, made from hand carved oak taken from the bark of local trees and the sunlight from the gap in the roof hit the stone floor in a perfect round shape, a picturesque perfect resting area for the passage to the next stage of life. In attendance were the usual faces of our town. Our neighbours, a family of 4 had perched themselves in the far corner, trying desperately to control their 2 young boys who were screaming and yelling across the hall. I followed my parents as they shook hands with everyone and many of them bowed their head to my father in return as a mark of respect.

The women in Naghaar were strange, stranger once they saw girls that had reached the desirable age. They would watch a young girl, try to imagine the shape of her body and the thickness of her thighs because that was apparently an indicator of a perfect childbearing woman. None of it mattered to me though, it would be the seeking ceremony that would choose my husband, not me. I had no say. My father joined the rest of the members sat at the front of the Patlin. A row of arrogant men, holding their heads high and demanding every Naghaari walking by to bow their head to them. I followed my mother, who approached a heavily pregnant woman sat near the front. This woman looked tired; her brunette hair was pulled back in a low ponytail, but it looked messy as if it was done in a hurry. Her eyes were an intense brown but were lost in a sadness that she tried to mask. She wore a white hat low over her eyebrows. She breathed heavily, slowly, with one hand on her knee and the other on her stomach.

"I'm so sorry". My mother leaned in and kissed her delicately on her cheek, the woman didn't look up. I too did the same and pecked her slowly on the cheek. *This must be Mrs Roman.* I wouldn't have known she was the man's widow because of the shocking shade of pink she wore. Whilst they spoke, I stood to a side and scanned the room for Lucia. From the corner of my eye, she ran to me and threw her arms around my body.

Lucia was a short girl with round glasses and freckles on her cheeks. Lucia's family was well off but by looking at her, no one could not tell she was brought up in affluency. She always dressed in muted colours and plain designs. Every day she plaited her thick black hair in the same braid, and it was always positioned on the left side of her head. Lucia was a strange girl. She was loud and boisterous, and she had no awareness of being empathetic or understanding. But I was glad just to have someone to talk to and our friendship had thrived for the past five years. Granted, she was completely crude at the worst of times, and we fell out very often, but somehow, we always found each other again perhaps because our friendship filled the cracks in our lonely universes.

"How are you?" she asked, grinning like a child.

"I'm okay. You?"

"I'm alright, I suppose. Say, have your parents mentioned the seeking ceremony yet?"

"No. And I hope they don't. Just thinking about that makes me sick…"

"You can't avoid it" she blurted out. "You're going to get married soon".

I crooked my head to the side and raised an eyebrow at her.

"Seriously? There's no better way you could've put that?"

"I'm just stating the truth" she shrugged her shoulders and looked behind me. "Who's that?". She pointed behind us. I turned my head to a young boy standing by my mother's side. He was tall and slim, with light brown hair that was brushed back. However, I noticed how one small strand at the top of his forehead never quite stayed in the same place and it constantly fell in front of his eyes, so he had to keep pushing it back with his hand. His cinnamon-coloured eyes were soft, and the tip of his nose was tinged red as if he had been crying not long ago. He was clean shaven, but I noticed that a tiny sprout of light brownish hair had begun to form under his lips. He wore a moss green shirt, buttoned right to the top and grey trousers that were the kind of fabric that rustled every time he moved. He smiled at my mother, and the tiny dimples at the corner of his lips deepened when he did. It was the kind of smile that tried to hide an aching sadness, but I saw through it. It was an all too familiar sight, as it was the kind of smile I often saw in my own reflection.

"He's handsome" Lucia chuckled to herself. "I really hope we get a handsome husband!"

"What about his heart?"

"His heart? That doesn't matter. It's the face that matters" Lucia grinned.

"This is the problem" I muttered. "All anyone ever cares about is beauty. But a soul is a part of beauty if not the very essence of beauty"

"What are you talking about?" she sighed, still staring at the boy.

"That's not how the world should work" I said firmly. "This system...everything…gives so much importance to a woman's beauty and her ability to produce children. But have you ever thought about how lucky we are? Imagine you were born with a physical defect, didn't grow at the same height as every other girl, your brain didn't function in the 'normal' way, or you couldn't have children?"

"You know these words will get you into trouble. Your thoughts are too unshackled, you need to rein them in" Lucia mumbled directing her gaze away from the boy and to a far corner of the hall. I frowned at her, frustrated that she didn't share my opinion.

"Life is ok for us" she continued, "just be happy and stop complaining"

"Seriously?" I questioned. "This system doesn't bother you

at all?"

Lucia shook her head.

"We're almost sixteen Lucia. You do realise we're going to be part of the ceremony soon? How can we be happy with a man that sees our worth because of our beauty and not because of what's in our hearts?"

Lucia let out a loud groan.

"This is what exhausts me about you. Recently you've started expressing these thoughts and you'll end up getting me in trouble. Talia do not put yourself in a precarious position".

I looked down at my hands, trying hard to control my anger. She had no sympathy, no awareness, to her the world was just black and white and no other colours existed.

"Those Pariah's are weaknesses in society. That's why they live there, and we live here" she spoke confidently.

"So, if I wasn't beautiful or healthy you would see me as a weakness?"

Lucia stared at me and then looked away. And that was the end of that conversation.

"Talia…!" I turned my head to my mother calling me over. I took a deep breath, trying to hide the way my anger flushed my cheeks. I turned away from Lucia and ran over to her.

"Talia this is Kalei…". I glanced at him, and he nodded his head in acknowledgment of my presence.

"I'm sorry for your loss" I spoke softly. "It's never easy losing a parent"

"Have you lost one?" he spoke with a firm brisk voice.

"N…no, luckily, but I understand…"

"Then you're not sorry" he mumbled, turning his head away in the opposite direction. I averted my gaze away from him, hurt that a stranger spoke to me in that way.

"Sorry" I whispered to myself. "Sorry for speaking".

How did I even turn out sane?

Talia

Under the thumb of a strict father, lost in the current of a subservient mother and a brother who thought it was best to leave our home for the comfort of another's. How did I turn out sane?

My brother Sarin was a quiet child. When we were younger, he would stay in his room quite often. He loved to draw pictures of nature and animals and mum used to keep a pile of those drawings in the kitchen cupboard. Since he left however, those drawings were stashed in the basement, collecting dust and losing their once vibrant colours. I wouldn't say I was a particularly loud child either, but I was definitely more boisterous than Sarin. Perhaps, that's why my father stamped his authority on me so much, in the fear that I would unreel out of control.

Growing up, my dad would take me with him to council meetings, and I would sit on his lap or in the corner of the room and groan and complain that I was bored. He would give me a plain parchment of paper and I would doodle on that until my small hands ached and I lost the passion for it. The council members would meet me, stroke my hair and remark how I would grow up to be a beautiful girl. Beauty meant income for them. I was a good source of potential future income.

The only time I could recall my father ever showing me love was when I was sick a few years ago. Unable to move, with burning skin and a hoarse voice, he came upstairs with a tray of hot tea and biscuits. He sat down beside me and lifted the cup to my lips. As I slurped, I remember looking at him and he smiled at me. It almost felt as if that was a dream because since then he never smiled at me again. I guess in some ways, my parents were afraid I would do what Sarin did. That I would leave the family and bring shame on the family name. The truth was, I did often think of leaving, wondering what life would be like in the city, but I didn't have the strength to escape. I would be too afraid of my own shadow to consider leaving the darkness of my home. So, for now, I must remain trapped, I must remain silent. If I did that, if I allowed myself to become a marionette, maybe then my father would love me.

Kalei

"I feel ridiculous wearing this colour. At my husband's funeral too!"

"It's okay mum. All the other clothes were too tight on

you, that's not your fault".

"What must people think of me? That I was dressed for a wedding and not a funeral. Who was that girl?" I looked towards the direction she was staring at; it was the girl from earlier.

"Nobody"

I had realised I was rude, and I regretted speaking to her in that manner. But in that short space of time, I had every single comment projected at me like missiles, and almost all of them were unpleasant and hurt like hell. Almost everyone had to comment that my mother was a widow, as if that information wasn't already obvious, and that her being a widow somehow made her incapacitated. I was lectured on how my presence was the only thing that would keep the home running and that I should pray that the child that my mother would very soon give birth to be a boy rather than a girl.

There my father's coffin lay, its brown wood glowing under

the sunlight, the wreaths' adding colour to the monotonous hall, yet that dead body held no weight here, because all everyone could do was talk about the weather, talk about their daughters or discuss interesting news that they received from the city.

That was what this funeral was.

My mother was the only daughter to her parents, both of whom died when she was young. She had an older brother, but my mother never mentioned him. But by the time she had lost her mother, just a few years after losing her father, she had already married my father, and she believed he would bring her the consolation she so desperately needed. They had a loving marriage.

Even on the day my father got his job in the city, she promised that she would stand by him. She coped well the first few months. She missed him desperately, but she quickly got used to being alone with me and during that time we bonded enormously. Being around only my mother, I began to rely on her for everything.

When I was twelve, going through emotionally and physically turbulent changes with no father to guide me through it, my mother sat me down and explained everything to me. From then on, I was comfortable enough to talk to her about everything.

As the funeral procession began, everyone took their seats. I placed my hand on my mother's lap, I could feel her legs shaking beneath my touch. I rubbed her lap hoping that any sort of friction would ease her distress. I turned my head and glanced around the room. There at the front, closer to the coffin than my own mother was, sat the council members. They sat with straightened backs; chins held up high as if their pride was the most important thing in the room. The only man missing was the leader, Makni Armis. I suppose his duty only reached the doors of the Patlin and not beyond. Behind them, a row of handlers was seated. Each one of them masked, sat still like statues. Suddenly, I felt a hand on my shoulder, I swivelled around and there sat Sami directly behind me.

Sami was short, he wore thick black glasses and wore a backpack that was larger than him. He lived a few streets away from me, and although we mostly saw each other in school, I felt like I had found a brother in him. He was attentive, caring and always had a smile on his face. I often wondered how Sami did it, how he could look at the world through a rainbow lens. Sami's mother had died many years ago, but he loved to hear me talking about mine. It was as if listening to my stories gave Sami room to imagine what having a mother would've been like.

We first bonded when I saw a quiet, reserved boy sat at the back of the class. I had not noticed him much, and he preferred to move in between crowds just to avoid being seen and drawing attention. Until one day, he was playing football in the playground with a bracelet that had the name 'Bozsik'.

"So, you like Bozsik?" I asked.

He looked at me, shocked that I had spoken to him.

"Y…yes" he stuttered".

"Me too" I smiled.

He pushed the ball with the sole of his feet, back and forward a few times.

Finally, he asked, "would you like to play?". And from there we began to bond.

Our thoughts became very much intertwined over time and

went far beyond the confines of Naghaar. We wanted to go beyond, beyond the forest and the desert and to explore the world outside. Sami heard that there were moving vehicles there, ones that would take you to places without you having to pedal anything. I heard that there were ways of communicating with others by hearing them over something called a phone. These new inventions absolutely boggled our minds, and he dreamt that by the time he turned 20, Sami would have enough money to go and live there.

"Where were you?" I whispered.

"Sorry" he mumbled. "Just…my father needed me".

I had not seen Sami since my father passed away but seeing him that morning took away every worry I had, because I knew after all the commotion, Sami would listen intently and find a way to make me smile. Sami was from the poorer side of town, he often tried to blend in with the rich at school, but his tattered shoes and mud-covered bag always revealed his true identity. He asked me for money many times, I knew he felt ashamed to and so many times he had expressed that he was extremely grateful that an upper-class boy like me became friends with a poor boy like him. Every time he said such things I looked him straight in the eye and I would hold out my little finger. Just like clockwork, he too would wrap his little finger around mine and we would say the words *adelfi*.

Brothers.

But, like everyone in the world, there was always something that they hid. Sami hid the truth about his father. I always heard stories about how Sami's father was cruel and lazy, and neighbours would say how they could hear Sami screaming in pain and his father yelling obscenities at him. Those screams would travel down the whole street and even though to this day Sami never told me, I saw the bruises he had on his arms that he tried so hard to cover up with the thick wool jumpers he wore.

Once the funeral was over, we all made our way to my house. There on the spread, the maids had put out a selection of breads, fruits, and fresh juices. There was a chatter around the halls of the home, almost every corner of the home was filled, even though our house was spacious, it felt so cramped that the front door had to be left open like a floodgate. As I weaved through the groups, I took one glance over at my mother who was sat with her feet up and then I made my way upstairs, hoping that I would find some relief from the sea of faces.

Leaning on the banister was the girl from before. She looked lost in thought, as if her mind was in an alternate dimension. She held half a cup of juice in one hand, but she grasped it so lightly I was afraid it would slip out of her hands and spill on some unsuspecting Naghaari below. She wore a white dress, pristine, with not a single crease. *She must be wealthy* I thought. Her hair was long and thick, falling to her hips and curling at the tips. Her eyelashes were long and thick, and her brown eyes were like coffee, something about them were delicate. After looking at her for a minute, I thought to myself that she was indeed beautiful.

A kind of beauty that was seldom seen in Naghaar. The women here were usually wildly dressed, especially the rich, in vivid bright colours and boisterous designs. But she was simple, and it was then I told myself that I should apologise for the way I spoke to her before.

"Excuse me" I cleared my throat, and she jumped a little like she was bought back to reality. Her eyes widened as if she was surprised. "I just wanted to say I am sorry for the way I spoke to you. I…I just have a lot going on. I didn't mean to come across like that".

"I…it's okay". Her voice was soft and peaceful, a perfect match to her pretty complexion. "I'm sorry if I offended you".

"No" I quickly interjected. "You didn't offend me at all. I was just not in the right frame of mind".

"It's a lot" she gestured to the large crowds below. "I'm sure it's hard".

I sighed, turned my body and leaned my elbows on the banister so that I was by her side. Almost close enough to touch.

"Talia, right?"

She nodded.

"Let me reintroduce myself properly. I'm Kalei Roman".

"Laris Roman's grandson?" she asked with a quizzical brow.

"Hmm" I replied. "Yes".

"Right…"

"Don't be afraid of me" I reassured her.

"No, I'm not scared. When you live in such an oppressive world you no longer fear being oppressed, you fear being loved".

She looked down, swivelled the juice in the glass and gulped the liquid down her throat in one go and placed it on the floor beside her feet.

"Do you have any brothers or sisters?" I asked her after a moment of silence. She shook her head.

"You? Your mum's expecting right?"

I nodded.

"I'm sure you will be an amazing brother. I'm sure it must be exciting being a brother for the first time" she smiled slightly; her eyes crinkled at the side.

"How come I've never seen you before?" I asked, surprised that this was the first time I set eyes on her.

"I don't go out much. Well, I'm not allowed out much, except for school".

Naghaari high school, was separated, the older part of the building, with its rusty door hinges, broken windows and limited furniture was the girl's side of school. Strictly no male students were allowed there. As for the male students, we were in the other building, which had been updated recently. Its tall columns and stoned walls were pretty features that too reflected the pretty interior. Immaculate white walls and solid oak tables and chairs were just some of the privileges we got. The only females that were allowed to attend school were daughters' or direct relatives to council members. That is how I knew Talia must've had a brother, father, or uncle that was a council member. But the general rule was that once girls were married off, they were very rarely allowed to go back into education by their husbands and thus very rarely seen at all.

"Tell me something about yourself…anything".

She scrunched her face as she thought of something to say. "I love nature" she chuckled. "Not very interesting but I love the trees. I love the sound they make when the wind blows, and I love the smell of fresh rain".

"Interesting" I smiled.

"Kalei…" she paused before she spoke again. "How are you feeling?"

I didn't respond.

"I mean, with everything going on. How are you doing?".

"I…I'm not sure" I hesitated. "I don't think it's sunk in completely yet".

"Were you close to your dad?".

"It depends on what you define 'close' as being". I sighed loudly. I could feel that her gaze was firmly latched onto me. I must admit, it made my knees buckle.

"I never really had many chances to sit with him and talk with him you know? He was so busy with work that I felt as if we were just humans he passed time with. Well, my mum and him were always close. But with me, I don't think I felt what I was supposed to feel around him. There was a big fuss with him. Everyone respected him for his work, but I always thought, a man's legacy should be his family".

"My dad's legacy is the council. That's all he cares about" she rolled her eyes. "Like you, I gave my soul to feel loved by him, but…" she took a deep breath and then stopped talking.

"You will find a man that loves you one day".

"I don't think so" she laughed inwardly. "I'm a girl. In this world, we don't get to feel loved, we get to feel owned". Suddenly she snapped her mouth shut as she if she was ashamed of what she said.

"I need to go…" she stammered. She quickly pushed her hands off the balcony and fixed her eyes on the stairs.

"You don't need to be afraid of me" I quickly spoke. "I may be a Roman, but you don't need to be afraid".

"I'm sorry" she said quietly. "I just…I don't trust any man

and you being a Roman I'm just…wary".

"Then let me tell you what I really think. There is something in a woman that a man will never have and because he can't have it, he does everything he can to take it away. The only way a man knows how to keep his power is to use what he has of his power to control her. A silent, limp toy is a useless one, right?".

"Wait…wait…" she took a step back, shaking her head in disbelief. "You're Laris Roman's grandson? I don't understand. You're supposed to be the essence of the system…it's in your blood…"

"Just because it's in my blood doesn't mean it's a part of me. You're the only one I've admitted this to, but I…I hate the system. And I hate it even more that I am attached to it…Please don't tell anyone this!" I implored. "I've never said this out loud".

She smiled at me, a smile that was vaster than the Indian Ocean.

"Wow…" she breathed. "Your secret is safe with me. But why are you telling me this?"

I paused, wondering whether I should lie through my teeth or just admit to her that there was something comforting about her.

"I…I'm just saying that's all…".

"Well…once your mother has her baby, if you ever need a babysitter, I'm happy to help!" she snickered. "I think I've found my first male friend!"

I smiled back at her. For the next hour we spoke about everything our life consisted of. Time passed quickly and because of her, the memory of my father's funeral wasn't as painful as I was afraid it would be.

That was the first time that I met Talia Arman.

The meeting that changed everything

Talia

Kalei had been called back downstairs by his mother and as he turned to walk away, he looked back at me, and I waved at him. I stood silent for a moment, surprised that in my fifteen years of living, I had finally felt what I thought was…attraction? I mean I didn't know what it was but the strange tingly feeling in my stomach told me that Kalei may have just started something either dangerous or something downright exhilarating.
He believed in the worth of women; I could see in his eyes that he had felt powerless and that something in him wanted to change that. But, then again, he was a Roman,

could I really associate with someone like him? Regardless of whether he believed in the allotment system or not, he was a clone of his grandfather. One day he would be a part of the very group that condemned us all to this prison. And what then? How could I see myself with someone who may one day turn against me and use his authority to detain me in purgatory? I had too many thoughts, too many feelings that I tried to suppress, and then I caught myself smiling.

Talia…you need to stop…

"Were you just talking to Kalei Roman?" I jumped and swung my head around to see Lucia standing behind me. "N…no…I mean yes but I was giving my condolences…"
"You were giving your condolences?" she raised her eyebrows at me. "Whilst laughing and blushing?"
"No" I quickly dismissed her. "I wasn't blushing".
"Look Talia I know he's handsome but he's a Roman. Men like him are arrogant and soulless. Don't talk to him".
"Lucia seriously? Weren't you ogling him not long ago?

There's no harm in talking to him!".

Lucia shook her head and folded her arms across her chest. "Don't say I didn't warn you. He will break your heart one day".

Kalei

"Four hours Kalei!" Meira screamed. "Four hours I was up there! I couldn't even see dad's body!".

Meira paced the room, her brown eyes glowing with an intense anger I had never seen before.

"I'm sorry" I spoke as calmly as I could. "You know why…"

"I've had enough of you and your excuses! You say you want to protect me from all the men out there but the worst man of all is you!"

"Meira, please understand! Naghaar won't accept you! You'll be branded as a Pariah!"

"I would rather be an outcast than be your sister….".

She stormed up the stairs and slammed the door behind her. Her words hurt. But lately she had been trying to hurt me more. It was working. I turned away and walked over to where my mother lay on the sofa. I bent down, placed my hand on her cheeks and wiped her tears.

She had lost the baby two nights ago. She had pushed and pushed and the moment he was born, he was born not breathing.

It was hard to describe the moment.

My mother was wailing, desperately trying to hold her child but the doctor pulled him away from her, frantically pressing on the little boy's chest in the hope he would take his first breath. Just a few days after she buried her husband, she lost her son. I wish I could un-recall how she screamed at the doctor not to take away the last piece she had left of her husband. I couldn't bear to see her that way, and for two whole days she cried so much that her head burned, her eyes were blood shot and her body trembled.

I did everything I could to tend to her, the maids watched her every minute of the day and every time I asked them whether she smiled once, they shook their heads and answered that they thought she'd never smile again. Meira had come downstairs in the early hours of that horrible night, trembling, and shaking, covering her ears to block out the screams mother made. For the first time in a long time, she wrapped her arms around me, and I softened into her, hoping that time would slow down so that I could feel her embrace for much longer. The doctor had ordered her to rest until the bleeding had stopped, and the doctor promised he would come back in a week to check in on her.

"Mum, you need to eat…"

She didn't reply. She stared at the ceiling blankly. "Mum?"
"What is the point of eating when I am only feeding myself?".

"Mum…"

"I carried a life for so long and I couldn't even bring him into this world. I failed as a mother".

"No mum" I shook my head. "It's not your fault".

"Your dad will hate me now" she began to cry. "He will hate me for not being able to bring his child into this world!".

"Mum…why would you say that?" I pleaded.

"It's not your fault mum" I repeated. "It's not your fault".

I wanted to scream in anger, yell and curse but all those feelings stopped the moment they hit my throat. And for the rest of the night, they stayed there, like a cancerous lump, seeping into my blood, infecting every part of my body. But these feelings were untreatable. I didn't know what to do. The only thing I could do was hold my mother through the night, listening to her call out to her deceased child. All I could do was hold her tight, watch the colour drain from her eyes and listen to her question why she had to lose her best friend and child in a matter of a few days.

The place by the meadow

Talia

"Mr Roman's wife lost her child. It was a baby boy" my mother said. I straightened my back, sat upright, shocked by what I heard. Just a few days before Kalei talked about being a big brother. I couldn't imagine what he would be going through, and in such a short space of time, losing a dad and then losing a brother.

"Is there a funeral?" I asked.

"Of course, it's a boy".

I frowned, anger searing inside of me. I could feel the blood rush to my cheeks.

"Can I go?" I asked.

"Why would you want to go to a baby's funeral?" my mother retorted.

"I think it'll do her good" mumbled my father from the other side of the room. "She needs to meet some families, make herself known. She is approaching sixteen soon".

I rolled my eyes, of course that's the only reason they want me to go. To show my face, to show off my 'assets' and what I could provide for the potential men of Naghaar. I took a deep breath, it didn't matter, I was glad they were allowing me to go. I needed to see Kalei again. I needed to be there for him.

It felt like déjà vu all over again, back in the same house I was in just a few days before. This time though, there were only a few Naghaari's, the house was almost empty and this time I could clearly see the colour of the floorboards, the wallpaper, and the mantelpiece decorations. There were no family pictures, and the white floral wallpaper was blindingly white and peeling in the corner. The mahogany floorboards had dents and scratches that for a family as wealthy as the Roman's was quite surprising. There were wet patches in almost every corner of the ceiling and the windows were filthy that you could scrape the black dust with your finger.

I searched the room for his face, going from one room to another. As the funeral was for a baby, the body wasn't placed in the Patlin. Instead, the coffin was meant to be kept at the home of the family for two hours before being carried to the graveyard by six men of the family. The rest of the family would then follow the coffin beating a traditional Naghaari drum made from snakeskin and oak. As I walked into the room next to the kitchen, my eyes fell on the coffin that was the size of a shoebox. I realised that only a single man would have to carry that, that's how small it was, and that man would have to be Kalei.

He was sat on the sofa; his hands were clasped together, and he was staring down at his feet. I couldn't see his mother anywhere. I approached him and sat down. He turned his head, and then smiled at me with his tear-filled eyes.

"Talia…I didn't think I'd see you…"

"I wanted to come…" I smiled at him. "Are you okay? Stupid question…" I shook my head. "Of course, you're not…"

"I don't know what to do" he cried. "My mother has shut herself up in her room. I feel useless…"

At first, I hesitated but then I slowly lifted my hand and placed it on his. To my relief, he didn't flinch or retreat. There was a warmth that radiated off his skin and for a moment I could've sworn I felt his fingers squeeze mine for a millisecond before they relaxed once again.

"When's the burial?" I asked.

"Not for another hour and a half".

"Then do you mind if I take you somewhere?".
He looked at me intently, scanning my face and wondering if I meant it and then he nodded. I could see he was overwhelmed and that he had no desire to stay in the house.
More than anything he needed an escape.
"Come" I whispered. I held out my hand and without hesitation he took it. His fingers wrapped around mine, fitting perfectly as if they were meant to be one.

We walked for a while, crossing into the forest that stretched out around the town. The branches stuck to my burgundy dress; leaves crunched beneath my shoes. He followed me closely behind, his hands dug deep in his pockets and his gaze to the floor, he didn't say a word. And I didn't push him to. Crossing the forest floor, we came to a clear small bright opening where the trees here were thinner, sparser and the mud had now disappeared and had become more like sand. Ahead of us was the meadow, the same one I once used to play in. Tears formed in my eyes the moment I set eyes on it; it brought back all those happy memories that reminded me of my girlhood.

I wanted to bring Kalei here because it was the one place in the whole of Naghaar that felt isolated, peaceful and where no one could see your vulnerabilities. Although the meadow was not like it used to be, the peace and stillness remained there. In the far distance, the same willow tree stood tall. Its' drooping branches, covered in bright green limp leaves created an umbrella of cool shade underneath. Its' jagged chocolate coloured trunk was rough to touch, and its' gentle rustling softly entered my eardrums in beautiful waves. Every time the leaves moved, the smell of wildlife, the exact kind of freshness that one would expect, would pleasantly enter my senses and it would widen my perception with its' immeasurable greenness.

Kalei finally looked up, observed his surroundings, and then he smiled. My heart fluttered.

"I used to always sit under that tree" I pointed to it. "The leaves sort of hid me, I guess. I thought you might like it here; I know I loved it".

"It's beautiful" Kalei whispered under his breath. I smiled to myself reassured that I had managed to do something right.

"You've got leaves and mud all over the hem of your dress…I'm sorry…" he shook his head ashamedly.

"You don't need to be sorry. I've got a million dresses. Come, I have a surprise for you…".

There was a part of me that wanted to slowly reach out and clasp my hands around his and lead him to where I wanted to take him. But I was afraid, afraid that if I touched him, he would push me away. So, I swivelled my body and continued walking, glancing back to make sure he followed.

Kalei

I watched as Talia stroked every blade of grass with her fingertips as she walked by, and with every step she took she scanned every inch of the sky with her exquisite eyes as if she had never seen daylight before. I knew with just the way she scoured the surroundings, and with the way her smile reached her ears, that this place had touched a part of her soul and that she was for sure a kindred spirit with the natural world. She looked down at my hand and I wanted to tell her that she could take it if she wanted to, I *wanted* her to. But after a brief second of hesitation, she turned away and continued to walk. As we approached closer to the tree I noticed a large piece of fabric, pale blue in colour and with small daisies printed on them draped on the floor just behind the tree trunk. On top of the cotton fabric were baskets of food, freshly baked rosemary bread, sweet strawberry jam and an assortment of berries, strawberries, blueberries, and a small jar of fresh milk. Talia stopped in her tracks and turned to smile at me. My heart pounded, like the fast-rushing Ondas river, it filled me with a kind of worth I had never felt before. She looked at me, back down at the fabric and then back up at me again. I stood, with my hands clasped behind my back and shook my head in complete awe at her kindness. She had prepared it all for me.

"Talia…why…?".

"I wanted to give you something to smile about. I know how hard the last few days have been for you".

"But how did you get it here?"

"That's a secret I'll never tell…" she tapped her nose with a sly smile.

"Tell me!".

She laughed, clearly amused by my confusion. "Gracie. I had her prepare everything the moment I found out about the funeral. The rosemary bread I made myself! The first time I've ever cooked anything! And she hired two local maids to take the food here and set it up whilst I walked to yours. I would've never been able to leave the house with baskets of food!".

"Did anyone ever tell you how kind you are?".

"Come on!" she yelled like a little child. "Let's eat!".

She crossed her legs, folded her arms, and waited for me to join her. I chuckled softly and then ran over to her and sat beside her, my shoulder almost touching hers.

"There used to be thousands of flowers here" she said as if she was speaking to herself. "It was like a sea of colour…now it looks so plain here, not as many flowers as there used to be".

She reached out for the breadbasket, took one herself and offered the other pieces to me. She then grabbed the basket of berries, took a handful herself then offered the rest to me.

"Kalei" she said so quietly that I could barely hear. "I'm so sorry about everything. I know that nothing or no one could ever take away the pain you're feeling. I was thinking earlier, that although life can seem so cruel, in harshness sweetness can be found".

"You know Talia that we barely know each other" I said. "But why does it feel like I've known you my whole life?".

She smiled and lowered her gaze to the ground. I was sure it was the first time she must've blushed because it was like the first bloom of spring, only in this case she was a single blooming rose in a barren land.

After a few silent seconds I spoke again. "I'm only telling you this because I trust you…" she looked at me, tucked a strand of hair behind her ear and leaned in.

"I have a sister…"

"I don't understand…"

"Her name's Meira. She's fourteen. We had kept her hidden for all these years because she…she has a physical deformity on her face".

My heart was pounding; I was afraid she would see me as a monster for hiding my sister or see me as a liar. Did I trust her too soon? I couldn't read her expression, she looked afraid and worried as if she was seeing eyes in the trees watching us.

"If anyone found out about Meira, I would lose her" I continued, hoping that my words would somehow convince her to side with me. "She would be branded and sent to the zone. Everything I've done is to protect her but now she hates me. She hates me for taking away her freedom".

I could feel tears welling up in my eyes, but I sniffled, and held them back. It was as if saying it out loud was more difficult, it felt as if saying it out loud made me feel like more of a beast. But then I felt her hand rest on my shoulder. It was a delicate touch, barely any weight to it but it radiated serenity and kindness. I looked up at her and I could see she was affected by it too.

"You wouldn't be taking away her freedom because there was never any freedom to begin with. I don't blame you for it. In fact, I admire you even more. So many men have branded the women of their family, but you protected her all these years".

I sighed, relieved that she felt the same as me, that she understood me.

"My mother is devastated. She barely speaks or eats. I don't know what to do".

"I'm sorry. Grief is unpredictable…how has Meira never been seen?"

"There's a small compartment my dad built that is just above the bathroom. There are some hidden stairs and then she goes in there every time we have guests around. She's never opened the curtains, seen the daylight or felt the breeze".

"I understand why you feel guilty, but Meira would struggle in the Pariah zone. She would be belittled, have hardly any clothes, food and would have to work dirty jobs for the rest of her life. Though she may not see it yet, you're saving her from something much worse".

For a few minutes, we sat still.

"Talia…I know I'm a Roman. I know that any connection to me may seem impossible for you right now. But…there's something so special about you. Something I don't want to let go of".

Her eyes twinkled, and her gaze softened.

"I don't care about your bloodline Kalei. The moment you told me you respected women was the moment I knew my fate was already sealed with yours…"

I was in a cocoon, safe, warm and she was the wings on my back. I had never believed it was possible to fall for someone almost instantly, but I did. I was falling for her.

"The world feels black and white" Talia sighed twiddling the fabric of her dress between her fingers. "There is so much darkness here"

"Yes, but even in darkness it is still possible to find colour.

Talia, we are the colour in it. I want to be in the rainbow that is in the colour of your smile".

She smiled and blushed and pulled her hand away from my shoulder. Before she could retreat in embarrassment, I pulled her hands and clutched them into mine. I pulled them close to my chest, and leaned in so her face was inches away from mine. I gently ran my fingers through her hair, the strands were soft and silky. Her hair smelt of warm vanilla. But more than anything, the connection that was between the skin of our hands was like a bright, warm ember in an intense snowstorm. I could feel the heat radiate off her cheeks. I could see every line, every beauty spot on her perfect canvas. I parted my lips to speak, I wanted to tell her everything I was feeling in the moment.

"I'm scared" she whispered.

"Of what?"

"Of falling in love…"

"I'm afraid it's too late for me already" I smiled. But before we could lean in any closer, a single raindrop fell onto my cheek. Then one, then two, then three. And before we knew it rain had begun to drench the food, our hair, and our clothes.

I quickly stood up, pulling Talia to her feet. "Come on" I pulled at her arms to try and find shelter before she was drenched to the core. But she stood firmly in one place.

"No"

"What?!" I was yelling now, trying to raise my voice above the sound of the rain that was heavily pelting the ground, trees and leaves. I could feel water trickle down my back, into my shoes and I shivered with the uncomfortable way my clothes began to stick to my skin. Talia skipped away from me, stood in the middle of the meadow, raised her arms in the air, tilted her head back and closed her eyes. She spun around in pure happiness, twirling, embracing every single drop on her face.

Her hair was now soaking wet, sticking to her back and to her face. But she had no care in the world. She didn't care that her bare legs were dripping and covered in mud, she didn't care that she had no jacket on and that her arms were completely uncovered. She spun, and laughed and screamed with ecstasy, and I watched in awe at the way she lived in that moment. I was confident that she would take my heart away and never give it back. I loved the way the rain hit her face, dripping off her long eyelashes and reddening her cheeks. I loved the way she moved her feet, light as an angel, barely touching the ground. I loved the way she spun in her maroon dress as if she was a radiant carousel in the middle of the midnight desert.

"Come on!" she screamed in joy.

"No" I shook my head, shoving my hands in my soaked

pockets, that felt as if they had shrunk in size. She stopped for a brief second and then continued to dance in the middle of the meadow.

The truth was, I didn't want to join her because I just wanted to look at her. Yet the small voice in my head told me, God willing, that I had a lifetime ahead of me to look at her but only a few moments to feel this for the first time. So, I took a deep breath and ran to her, threw my arms around her waist and spun her around. She screamed and laughed. Little did she know that I saw a beauty in her eyes that only she couldn't see, and a heavenly melody in her laughter that only she couldn't hear. My fingers traced the skin around her stomach, I leaned my chin on her shoulder and for those moments that we danced in the rain I forgot the broken world that I left behind me.

I forgot every single thing when I was with her.

Back to reality

Talia

It all felt like a dream….
The way Kalei looked at me, the way he held my hands and the way he spun me around and danced with me. I was afraid, so afraid of everything we would yet be. But now as I walked back home, that moment had become a memory, one that I would cherish for the rest of my life. This was how it was supposed to feel like…falling in love…

I loved every part of him, the way his brown eyes glinted even in absence of sunlight, the way his hair had become so wet that it drooped over his eyes, and his hands…how soft they were, how gentle, the way my hand fit into his as if they were always meant to be one singular entity. But now that it was over, I finally began to feel the sensations around me. I felt my body shiver, the goosebumps on my arms and legs had receded and I could feel the way my dress clung to my skin as if it was another layer on my skeleton.

Everyone in Naghaar had retreated into their homes, and there I was weaving through the streets, walking briskly to avoid any unwanted looks at my unkempt appearance. I never thought about what my parents would say. What excuse could I give for the way I looked? Although my heart was still pounding, it was no longer beating in happiness but rather in fear. And worst of all, I would be turning sixteen soon. What would I do when that moment came? How could I watch another man buy me like a piece of furniture when my heart was now in the echoes of Kalei's footsteps?

After that moment, Kalei had rushed back home in time for the burial, promising he would see me again very soon. His demeanour had once again looked broken, knowing he had to go back and finish what he tried so hard to avoid.

Knowing he had to go back to looking at his grieving mother and then feeling guilty because he experienced a fraction of happiness on the day his mother couldn't.

"Are you out of your mind?!" I sprang back in fear, startled with the voice behind me.

"God, Lucia! You scared me!".

She stamped over to me, her eyes examining every part of my body, scowling, and shaking her head in disappointment.

"You went to see that boy, didn't you?" she folded her arms aggressively across her chest.

"Kalei. And no…I didn't…I went to the funeral and happened to see him there. That's all."

"So you just happened to be soaking wet and flushed at the cheeks?"

I shrugged my shoulders in the hope she would accept my lies. I couldn't tell her; I knew she would only scold me for the way I acted.

"I'm not going to say this again Talia. He's the grandson of Laris Roman. You do realise he'll be a council member soon!"

"It's not his fault who he's associated with" I snapped, completely fed up with the way Lucia always talked down at me. "I'm enjoying my life, okay? Since when do you care about the system anyway? I think I'm falling in love…"

She snorted and let out a loud laughter, a mocking laughter.

"Love. You don't even know what that is…"

"Just because you want what I've got doesn't mean you try and take it away from me. If you were really my friend you would be happy for me…"

She stared at me, her eyes softened slightly.

"I'm saying it for you. I just want to protect you. Anyway…I won't have to try and take away anything from you. Your parents will do that…probably on your sixteenth birthday."

She turned and disappeared around the corner. Where were the times when everything was so simple? The times I used to sleep over at Lucia's house when the only worry we had was whether our mothers could hear us laughing under the duvets. The times when we used to pluck petals off flowers and collect them in small glass jars because we thought they were magic. The times I could disappear into the forest, listening to the sounds of the chirping birds whose small distant shapes met the tall, motionless foliage and vanished into its greenery. I had so many thoughts running through my mind and so much to answer for. With a palpitating heartbeat, I turned into the street where I lived.

"What happened to you?!" my mother yelled as soon as I entered the house. "You're completely drenched!"

"Err…yeah. It started raining heavily at the graveyard" I lied.

"Why did you go to the cemetery?" she questioned angrily. "It's not proper for a woman to be seen there. Are you out of your mind? We said go to the funeral at their home, not follow them to the graves…"

"Sorry" I mumbled, hoping she would accept my story.

"Go, get cleaned up" she grumbled, "Stupid useless girl".

I nodded and took a deep breath, she believed me.

As I walked up the steps, and down the hallway, I opened the door to my room to find Gracie waiting for me. She smiled, revealing her crooked, yellow teeth. It was such a pure smile.

"So…?" she asked, clenching her teeth in excitement. I

closed the door softly behind me, running up to her and leaning into her to whisper.

"Oh Gracie it was magical!"

She giggled, and I laughed too, but she quickly put her finger to her lips so that we didn't make too much noise.

"Oh my love. I'm so happy for you!".

I flopped onto the bed and stared at the ceiling. I couldn't stop smiling, I couldn't stop seeing his face in my mind.

"Will you finally tell me who he is?"

"Gracie…it's…Kalei Roman"

"Laris Roman's grandson?" she questioned worryingly.

I nodded.

"This is not good Talia" she shook her head and slowly stood up. "It's not good".

"Why?"

"Why? Talia, to be a council member's wife is like imprisonment. It won't suit your lifestyle at all!".

"I'm not going to marry him Gracie" I joked.

"Then why are you wasting your time? Why are you wasting his? Most of all, why are you risking your heart like that?".

"Gracie, I'm just getting to know him. I mean, I might marry him in the future…I don't know" I shrugged my shoulders. "He's really nice Gracie. He's not like the other council members!".

"How do you know that?" she furrowed her eyebrows. "Because he told you that? Men are liars Talia. I've taught you better than this!".

She had become angrier, and she began to walk back and forth in front of me with the only a certain level of pace her frail body could allow.

"Talia listen to me. If you want to be with him, you do it the right way. Ask him to bid for you at the seeking ceremony".

"No" I shook my head.

Gracie sat beside me and put her delicate arms around my

shoulder.

"My darling I know you've been avoiding this conversation but you're turning sixteen soon. Does he even know? And then what? What if some other man gets you? All this, you, him, is all pointless then".

"No. I...I can't ask him to do that...He's only known me for a few days, I can't ask him to bid on me as a last resort and then expect him to be happy to marry a woman he barely knows!".

"Talia, if he is as genuine as you say he is, he would make sure that you become his. And maybe then, you can have all the wealth and privileges of a council member's wife without feeling imprisoned".

She took my cold hands which had dried now, and she stroked them with her rough fingers, the smell of paprika lingered on her stained apron.

"You're like my daughter Talia. I was never blessed with any of my own, but I see you as mine. And as your mother,

I want you to be happy. I don't want you to marry because you were sought out at the highest price. My love, please talk to him…"

"Not yet Gracie. Not yet. I just want to enjoy our time together before I ruin it by asking him to throw away his future to save mine. I want to stay in this dream. I want to stay in the meadow…"

Kalei

I vowed that I would never forget the day I finally saw my mother smile again. What a graceless ageing beauty she was. She was out in the garden pouring water over the flowers, and I watched from the window as the corners of her lips turned up and her eyes crinkled like a little child. It had been so just over two weeks since she lost the baby. It had been difficult, for both of us, but I never could tell her just how lonely I felt without her. Although I was seventeen, every time she opened her arms to embrace me, I felt as if I was a little boy again, running to her as if it was the first time since residing in her womb, that I felt her skin connect to mine.

The past few days she had slowly regained her strength, started eating again and yesterday was the first full day that she didn't shed a single tear. It finally seemed that she had found the light within her; but the neighbourhood women always dimmed her light. There were rumours circulating that she had lost her mind since her son's death, the doctor of Naghaar had gossiped and spread vile rumours that he saw her acting possessed and deranged. There were words and murmurs because no one had seen her since the funeral and supposedly she was incapable of talking to other humans without bursting into tears. She had received letters from the neighbourhood, advising her to admit herself to the asylum, for her own 'betterment'. She was distressed, and even though she had smiled, a few hours later she was soon back to her usual self, crying, talking to herself, having private conversations with shadows in the corner of the house and whispering about things I never understood.

She never spoke about the child or about dad. Every time I did ask, she shut me out immediately. Meira had come down, but she brushed past me, sat on the sofa and began to read a book.

"Meira…come on…" I urged her as I went over and kneeled beside her.

"Not until you let me out of the house" she murmured into

the pages of her book.

"Why can't you understand?" I was frustrated now. "You're not a child. What part of the whole system, the Pariah zone don't you understand?!".

Meira threw her book down and glared at me. The black strands of her hair had fallen out of her short ponytail and fell in front of her face.

"Mum doesn't talk to me. I can't stand being around you. Why am I a prisoner?"

"Meira, I don't understand. Only the last few months you've started acting like this. You need to understand, mum needs time to heal…"

"I've had enough. I'm sick of being kept in like an animal. How long do you expect me to be patient? Am I going to stay in the walls of this home until I die? Whilst you go out, anywhere and everywhere you want. You can marry who you want, have children and never be scrutinised. If f I got a knife and slit your lip, they wouldn't see that as deformity, they would see that as unfortunate. But they wouldn't imprison you!".

She snatched the book aggressively and hid her face behind it in irritation.

"I understand you, Meira. I know it's difficult…" I sighed.

"You never hug me anymore. My love for you hasn't changed…I'm still your big brother…"

"Well my love has changed!" she spat. She slammed the pages shut and then ran upstairs again. I sat on my heels, still and quiet. I couldn't do anything right anymore. Meira resented me, in a way I never thought she would. And my mother had gotten lost in another universe and struggled to find her way back to this one. I was overwhelmed, I was drowning. I stood up, picked up my jacket and stepped out into the cold air.

I walked to Sami's house, after just a few minutes, I was at his doorstep. Before I could lift my hand to knock on it, I heard a piercing scream from behind the door. My heart froze. After a moment or two Sami's father let out a ghastly sound and then all I heard were silent sobs. I wanted to break the door down and see if Sami was okay, but I couldn't. I had no authority to do that, and Sami's father was a large man, he could easily break me in half.

I stood there for a while, until I felt like enough time had passed, I lifted my hand to knock. After a few moments of fumbling, steps and unlatching, Sami creaked the door open. His eyes were red, as if he hadn't slept and his hands were trembling against the door frame.

"Now…now's not a good time Kalei" he attempted to close the door before I stopped it abruptly with my hands.

"Sami…are you okay?"

"No" he whimpered.

That was the first time I saw him cry. He threw his arms around me and dug his face into my shoulder. The way he wept I could never forget. It was the sound of someone finally letting out years of pain in just a few short minutes. Here I stood with my best friend sobbing in my arms, a little sister who couldn't even look at me and a mother who was absent. How I wished I could change everything for everyone, but the truth was, even if my mother saw me as a man, to the world I was still a boy. And that made a difference. Unless I took the pledge. Unless I succumbed to the fate written for me. Only then could I save my family, by becoming a part of something I never wanted to be a part of.

Only we mattered

Talia

I had been walking on my way to school, thinking to myself that perhaps this would be one of the last few times I could do this. Who knew whether my future husband would allow me to study? Ever since that conversation with Gracie, I couldn't stop thinking about the seeking ceremony. I couldn't stop thinking about how I would navigate my relationship with Kalei in a way that wouldn't compromise his or my future. The thought sent waves of anxiety through the pit of my stomach.

As I crossed the street, I looked up to find Kalei waiting at the corner. He smiled at me, and I swear I stopped breathing for a few seconds. I looked around and quickly dashed over to him. He was leaning against a wall, one hand in his pocket and another draping the navy-blue school blazer over his shoulder.

"Kalei. What are you doing here?"

"Well, I remember you telling me about going to the girls' school and well, I just asked a random schoolgirl on the way here what time your classes start"

"So you're stalking me?"

"No…" he averted his gaze. "I was going to school too and I was just curious"

"Right…You do realise boys are not supposed to be on this side. Your entrance is down there" I pointed off to the far distance across the iron gate.

He nodded his head and pushed his body off the wall. He got his blazer, slipped his arms through it and fixed his collar.

"They won't say anything to me" he said confidently. "So,

does that mean you've snuck in here before? Possibly to meet other girls?"

"Of course. I have loads" he smiled cheekily.

I looked down at my shoes and then back up at him.

"How about we skip school?"

I gaped at him wide eyed.

"No Kalei! I've never missed school!"

"Please. For me?"

He looked at me deeply, and after a few seconds, I glanced behind and let out a huge sigh.

"This better be worth it" I muttered. He smiled widely and then gestured for me to follow him.

We took the back alleys that were littered with the town's rubbish and from time-to time animals skittered across or ran out of bins. I jumped and grabbed his arm tighter with every noise or flash of movement. I was terrified that my parents would see me and that would mean I would probably never be allowed to walk to school again. I walked closer to Kalei, and I could see from the corner of my eye that he wanted to laugh at the ridiculous way I was acting. We followed a sandy trail towards the back of town, I had never been towards this side, but it was much quieter and the more we walked, the less of the towns people crossed our path. The trail was soft and dry, and bits of grass spurted up in several places. Ahead of us was a small grassy hill, and I watched as Kalei took long strides, easily climbing up whilst I panted trying to keep up with him. Eventually we came to the top and I took a few moments to catch my breath before focusing my eyes on the view ahead of me.

It was the whole town of Naghaar from above. Every single street, narrow and wide, wavy, or straight could be seen. The market was completely bustling, with women carrying baskets of fruit and men walking ten paces ahead. Couples sat in their gardens, children played football using white grids drawn by chalk and students were talking and laughing in the school playground. It was chaotic and wild. Beyond that, in the very far off distance, barely visible, a thin line of gold reminded me that there was another world beyond the desert.

"Wow" I breathed. "I've never been here".

"I come here with Sami a lot. My best friend. Not many people know about it".

"So why have you brought me here?"

"Well you took me to your place, so I wanted to take you to mine".

He sat down on the ground and stretched his legs out in front of him. I did the same too.

"Sometimes we get so caught up in the world we forget that there are opportunities beyond". He looked over at me. "I want you to always remember that although here, your gender, your beauty, your worth is all dependent on the views of men, out there…" he pointed out beyond the town. "You're someone special. Promise me one day you'll escape this place and find your worth".

I was perplexed with the way he was speaking. "I…where's this coming from?"

"I'm a Roman, Talia. I…you're wasting your time with me".

I blinked my eyes and sat still for a moment. "How am I wasting my time? Because of your bloodline?!"

"Because I'm going to be a council member in just a few short months. You do realise, I…I can't associate with you after that. I'm taking the pledge. That's it".

I could see him watching me, waiting for me to reply, but I couldn't look at him. Although I knew that he would be a member soon, I somehow, maybe blindly, believed that it didn't matter. Not to us.

"I…I didn't realise you're…this soon…I thought I would have…. more time with you…" I sighed. "So what? It doesn't matter".

"It does matter" he raised his voice. "Once I'm a member I'm important. I can't drag you with me".

"What if I want to be with you?".

He turned to look at me, his eyes were sincere and still.

"Talia, why would you want to be with a council member? It would ruin your life".

"How?" I asked, frustrated that he was trying to end everything so quickly. He sounded just like Gracie.

"Because, you'll have to dress a certain way, act a certain way. You hate the allotment system but by marrying me, you'll automatically have to proudly represent it".

"I can pretend" I assured him. "I'm good at pretending".

"No!" he yelled, turning his face towards the view. "I won't ruin your life!".

"So, you're just going to pretend I never existed?".

I saw his chest rise and fall but he didn't say a word.

"Kalei, don't do this". I quickly put my hand on his, but he pulled it away. "Wha…why are you saying all of this?!". I could feel tears on the edges of my eyes.

"I'm turning sixteen soon anyway" I spoke bluntly. I didn't plan on bringing the topic up, but I knew I was being childish. I was trying to hurt him the same way his words did. But the truth was, I was just trying to mask the overwhelming grief I was feeling at the reality of it all. He shot his head towards me; I could feel his shock too.

"You're trying to hurt me too huh?" he said harshly.

I hastily dug my head into my arms. I felt his hand graze the small of my back, and he kept it there. We sat in silence and though there were no words, I could feel and hear everything he was thinking. He took my hand and shuffled his body closer to mine. I was hesitant at first, but I leaned my head on his shoulder and kept it there. I could feel his breath on my forehead and after a few minutes he lay back on the grass.

"Come" he held out his arms and gestured for me to join

him. I lay down next to him and placed my head on his chest. He wrapped his arms around my shoulders and squeezed me tight. I could hear his heartbeat against my ear. So soft, so comforting. I don't know how long we lay like that, holding each other but I knew that at that moment adoration carved paths through the flora surrounding my soul, and it felt as if my soul had been opened by Kalei. That path he carved would remain unblemished eternally. And regardless of our fears about the future, we were living in the present and we were enamoured. Everything he said suddenly dropped to the back of our minds. We never brought it up again. I don't know if that was a good thing or a bad thing. In a way, we knew that although we could possibly never have a future together, we wanted to enjoy the time we did have.

The future could wait.

We were more important. Only we mattered .

Wildfires

Kalei

I had returned her back to school by the time it had almost ended. As she turned to walk away, I couldn't help but feel I wanted to shackle her to me and never let her go again. But the truth was that I couldn't, no matter how much I wanted to. I had to become a member, I had to try and make the lives of my family just a little better. With the money I would get, I could ensure my mother received the best treatment, I could ensure Meira had everything she ever wanted. I could also ensure Sami's father could get imprisoned for the way he treated him. Status meant power. I could change so much.

But Talia and I…it could never be because I knew that she had fears about marrying. I knew she wished she could leave Naghaar to pursue dreams that she had not yet quite figured out. I couldn't give her that. I couldn't make her happy. And she deserved it. God, she deserved every piece of goodness in the world. And now she would be someone else's in a mere few weeks and I would have to stand back and watch the first girl that changed my heart, have her heart be taken by someone else.

Perhaps I could've bid for her at her seeking ceremony but, I didn't want to. She wasn't an item to buy. I wouldn't *buy* her. It just went against all my morals. And what then? She would be the unhappiest wife because everything in our marriage would be for others. I could never give her anything that was just ours. I could never forget how her eyes dropped into an intense sadness and I could never forget how the rest of the time we sat in silence. If that was the last time I would see her, I wished I could at least see her smile once more.

The moment I returned home, there was a letter addressed to me in the letter box. The writing was slanted, wobbly and there was no wax stamp on it of any kind. I ripped it open.

Kalei,

I write you this letter because I'm afraid. Talia cares a lot about you. She sees something in you she's never seen before and felt something with you she can't comprehend. But my son, if you care for her please release her. She will never be happy as a council member's wife. She needs to stop loving you so she can be given the chance to love someone else. She can't escape her destiny and I'm afraid to say you're not her future.

Let her go.

Gracie

Don't worry Gracie I thought. I've already let her go. Around a few weeks later, there was a knock at my door in the middle of the night. Mum and Meira were fast asleep, and I cautiously made my way down, careful not to wake them in the process. I was unable to sleep, tossing and turning, hoping that the cooler side of the bed might ease me to sleep. But it didn't. I rubbed my eyes and proceeded to open my front door in the darkness.

Talia stood there, her tear-soaked face and distressed eyes startled me.

"Talia?" I whispered. "What are you doing here?!"

"Kalei, please. I need to talk to you"

I pulled her inside the door and quickly locked it behind me. I took her by the hand and sat her down, I stared at her, waiting for her to speak. She began to sob uncontrollably, I was flustered, desperately trying to wipe the tears rolling down her cheeks with the tips of my fingers. She could barely speak.

"Kalei…" she whimpered. "They're taking me to the seeking ceremony in a few days. I had to see you before then…"

I looked at her completely bewildered.

"Talia, please" I begged. "We talked about this…"

"No!" she shot her hand up in front of her. "No, we didn't

talk about it. You said that we can't be together but why can't we? I can be a perfect wife! I can learn to cook and clean. I'll do everything that is expected of a council member's wife!".

"Talia!" I shouted in frustration pushing her hands down onto her lap. "You're making this more difficult than it has to be!". I quickly glanced around the room and reminded myself that I needed to control the volume of my shaky voice.

"Tell me you love me, Kalei!" she sobbed. "Please tell me!".

She was desperate, I could see that she would give anything to have just one more day before she had to face her reality. I stood up and began to pace around the room, scratching the back of my head in nervousness.

"I need you to bid for me…" she blurted out.

I stopped and turned to look at her. She could see I hated the idea.

"Talia…we've been through this. You're not an object Talia. I'm not going to buy you"

"I know Kalei. But it's the only way. Please!"

"Do you know what you're asking of me?" I was angry, confused, upset all in one. "You're asking me to be responsible for your happiness for the rest of my life. Your life would be for me to take care of. I would be condemning you to a hell that you can't possibly understand!".

"So that's it?" she shot up and approached me with anger. She frowned at me, her face just a few inches away from mine. "Everything we felt, everything we talked about was all just to pass time?".

I gritted my teeth. Her proximity to me was intoxicating. I wanted to have her and hold her. I wanted to take her vulnerabilities and wrap them in my embrace. I puffed out my cheeks and took a step closer to her.

"Talia" I said in an almost whisper. "It just can't happen. I…I felt so much with you. Just the thought of you drives me wild. But look at the world we live in. It's not for people like us…"

She took a step back and gently wiped her tears. She took a deep breath.

"Okay…" she breathed. "I won't bother you anymore…"

Before she turned to walk away, I clasped my hand tightly around her wrist and pulled her into me. Our lips connected for the first time. The world around us blackened and faded and it felt as if the air around us sparked and set on fire. We were two candle lights', untouched, glowing, dancing in our own light amongst the darkness of the room. Never did I think it was possible to feel this way. Never did I want to ever let her go again because it would mean I would have to let go of everything that made this moment. No matter how many days and weeks I tried to forget her, I simply couldn't. I was drawn to her, like a magnetic unstoppable force. And as we parted, I leaned my head against hers and realised that my eyes had opened a small dam and let a single salt stream escape from it.

"I promise, I would marry you in a heartbeat if I could. I'm so sorry." I breathed.

She didn't say a single word. She stepped back, looked at me one more time and disappeared out of the house, gently clicking the door behind her. I swear I heard my heart shatter, wasn't that what that sharp pain in my chest was? I tried to submerge my sadness.

"Talia!" I shouted out. I quickly followed her and ran out the door, carelessly yelling her name down the street. She swivelled her body around. I could see hope light up her face.

"I…" I gulped. I wanted to say that I loved her but instead the only words that came out of my mouth were "if you ever need me, I'll be under the willow tree every Sunday at 6am. If you ever need me".

What a ridiculous thing to say.

The seeking ceremony

Talia

At that very moment, I was being taken by my parents to the council chamber. I had never been inside before but judging by the people around me who were crying in happiness, they clearly hadn't either. In front of me was a large brown tepee. It was bigger than I had imagined, with red strings hanging down from each corner and underneath my feet was a soft red rug that travelled all the way to the opening of the tent. I lived on the quieter side of Naghaar, so the sights of bustling crowds, the smells of fresh bread and fruit and the fusion of the sounds of laughter and screaming were completely new to me.

Many people had gathered and were watching me with complete focus. I could feel all their gazes on me as I took one step forward. My mother was to my left and my father was walking a few paces ahead. I couldn't even begin to explain just how much my heart was racing under my skin and how clammy my palms were, but in that moment, it was like I was in another universe. One in which I didn't want to belong in. You see, although I was not yet sixteen, my parents sat me down a few nights before and told me how they wanted to secure a bid for me by the time I turned sixteen. I remember feeling numb, confused, anxious because although I had anticipated it, I hadn't expected it so soon. But even after I cried and begged them to give me another week before the ceremony, they didn't listen. And so that's why, for the first time in my life I snuck out of the house and ran to Kalei's home. I don't know why, but it felt as if it was the only thing I could do. But now here I was, walking through the gap in the tent and entering the council chamber. Kalei had given up on me and for some reason, I found that difficult to accept.

As I entered, the same red rug was on the ground and there were brown cushions scattered around in the shape of a large circle. In the middle of that circle was a larger brown cushion that was higher up and more intricately decorated than the others. I assumed that was Makni Armis' place. In front of every cushion there were small wooden trays that had books and quills on top of them. I looked up and noticed the sunlight peaking in through a circular hole right in the middle of the brown fabric, but other than that the place was eerily dark, with only a few candles propped up on the side oak cabinets. It was comfortably warm, and I gulped hard when I was told to wait there. The strangers outside had swarmed into the tent, and I tried to catch my breath in the human tidal wave. Why were all these people here? Where was Lucia? Everyone was informed that today would be my seeking ceremony.

A short old man walked out from a hidden opening to the left and cleared his throat. Everyone fell silent.

"We are gathered here today to witness the bidding of Talia Arman, daughter of Mr and Mrs Arman. Talia step forward".

Hesitantly I stepped forward, but I was quickly stopped.

"Shoes off" he grumbled.

I slipped off my black shoes, my legs were trembling under my long grey dress. They made me sit in the middle, right opposite the leader's seat. Within a few seconds, eighteen men came walking out. All of them were of various ages and sizes but all wearing the same menacing glare on their faces. In all my confusion I hadn't noticed my father slip out because he too had walked in with the rest of the council, wearing the same look on his face. I had grown accustomed to the fact that my father was on the council, but I had never really imagined what he looked like when he performed his duties. Apart from the day that Mr Roman's funeral happened, he usually kept his council life and his home life separate, I very rarely saw him in his attire. He didn't look like my father at all.

They all sat down onto their cushions and looked at me so deeply that I could feel my bones rattle in fear. My father looked through me as if I was a stranger which made my stomach turn in uneasiness. My mother was stood amongst the crowd, and I looked over at her, begging for her to cast me a comforting look. But just like my father, she looked right past me and was clearly more enamoured with being in the presence of the council and in anticipation of Makni Armis.

A minute passed, for what felt like an eternity of dread, and then everyone watched as Makni Armis walked in. He had a long white beard with small circular glasses. He held a wooden crutch and was helped along by a few of the members. They all bowed their head as he entered the circle and took a seat in front of me. From first impressions, he appeared to be a frail old man who had difficulty in lifting his limbs. But, inside that vessel of saggy skin was a man with the sharpest wit, disturbing level of greed and all the while sitting in his comfortable citadel of corruption. He had a large birthmark on his forehead, that was only partially covered by the tall hat he wore. He looked like he struggled to carry its weight.

So, it was him. He was the man who had the town tail him in admiration, throw money at his feet, he was Laris Roman's successor, and for sure carried Roman's vile ideals as he would've done.

Because of this system, I had to sit there and let the body I grew up in be handed over to be controlled by another man. In that small space, there was a collision of two forces, one with an insurmountable power on his frail shoulders and another with no power in her hands.

Makni Armis read out a list of rules and then told the first man to come in.

"How much will you pay for her?"

The price of a woman depended on many things. She must be slim, with pale skin and thick hair. Thick hair was assumed to signal the level of fertility. Women who were proportionately larger in size were often sold at very low prices, if they were lucky enough. For the men that did acquire these larger women, those men were very often from poorer families, and only needed these women for manual labour and childbearing. Women of a higher price would be sold to a man from a wealthier background, but there was no guarantee that she would have a better lifestyle. Yes, she had better clothes, shoes and jewellery. She had a whole beautiful house and huge gardens, but she too was expected to provide many children. But in such cases, they had maids to look after them, so in a way they were deemed *lucky*. And that's exactly what my parents wanted for me.

As for the men in the council, they were known to be flirts. From the moment a young girl was able to walk, they would scan her body, they would look at her skin and her eyes and confer between them whether she was going to have beautiful assets when she grew older. By the time I reached puberty, I very often found myself more conscious of my growing body and very often I would see Naghaar men gaze at me from top to bottom, with their eyes often falling and freezing at my chest. These men objectified women, and ironically, they casted out women for not meeting the beauty standards. Yet they still used those same women's bodies for their own satisfaction when they snuck into the Pariah zone. It never made sense.

And so, a young girl, so afraid of growing up and being sold out to the world, couldn't even feel safe in her own home first. Perhaps that's why I felt so safe around Kalei. From the moment I met him, his eyes fell on me in a respectful way. I didn't feel as if his eyes were undressing me or if he was thinking of vile things. I felt, no I knew, he saw me as a woman, a true woman, and that made me feel worthy. But it was all a waste. I would never feel respected like that again…

The pattern of bidding went on for an hour. One man after another came into the room and offered their bid. These bids were never disclosed to the bidders until after the ceremony. If one man came into the tent and offered less than what was offered before, he would simply be told, not enough, and sent home. The successful man would be the man who offered the largest sum of money that he could afford. Unfortunately, that man was Tamin.

He was a 32-year-old man. He glared at me with his scraggly beard, plump belly and stroked his chin with his dirty fingernails. He looked at me up and down and smiled repulsively. At one point I could see his eyes strip the clothes off my body, I could see in his eyes that he saw my body as his property and his possession, that he knew he could do with me what he liked. I was slim and tall, with thick black hair and pale skin. And so, I was deemed a perfect offering for the men of Naghaar.

Tamin offered 400 garoles and by the end of the exchange, Makni Armis shook hands with Tamin and congratulated him on his beautiful polished new China doll.

They called me a *China doll*.

A beautiful girl with porcelain butter like skin, who hidden in her, had much more to offer. In my mind, I had so much to offer. My kind heart, my grandeur outlook of the world and my love. But to them, I offered a chance to be under their submission. I offered a chance for them to bestow in me seeds of their manliness that would grow and only become a slave to their avarice. And what would be left of me? If I didn't die in childbirth, which so very often happened, I would be left living in the shell of my former self, having given everything to bring a child to the world that will only ever be the fathers' and not mine.

A doll was something I used to play with, I gave it time and attention because it was interesting, new, and fascinating. But, over time the doll lost its eye, the threads began to come undone until one day it was simply not appealing. And then the doll was either thrown away because it no longer provided a purpose, or the doll was given away at a fraction of the price it was brought. And that's what I was. A *doll*. Tamin's doll. I knew that right at that moment I was interesting and new to him, but one day Tamin would decide that I was simply tiresome and not enough. And that thought deeply troubled me.

My father beamed in happiness and stood up to shake Tamin's hands. Any hope I had was diminished into insignificant ashes. I had some hazy confidence that I would not get married at 16 and that maybe I would have the freedom to choose what I wanted or that maybe Kalei would come rushing in and save me.

But he didn't.

I wanted to scream and writhe in anguish, but I stayed silent because I had been trained to stay silent. I chewed my lips till they bled, it was the only distraction to the sound of applause around me. I refused to look up, I didn't want to look up.

I was successfully sought out.

A thought came into my mind, the first self-destructive one I had. Perhaps if I sliced my skin open, maybe then Tamin would withdraw his bid. Perhaps if I shaved my head and poured boiling water over my legs Tamin would be revolted and beg the council that he didn't want to marry me. I thought of everything all the while I was feeling nothing.

An empty shell

Kalei

Just a few days before, I had woken up to the sound of a loud shatter coming from my mother's room. I burst through the doors to find her sitting in the corner of her room, with her legs tucked into her chest. Her hair was dishevelled, her clothes were wrinkled, and broken glass was strewn all over the floorboard. She had her head in her arms, but she was silent.

"Mum?" I asked concerned.

I gently walked over to her being careful to not let the shards cut my bare feet.

"What happened?" I asked her.

She didn't move, she kept her head hidden in her arms. I glanced around the room, in the far corner was their wedding photo, the same one she had been looking at often. The mirror that sat on top of her dresser was half shattered, as if she threw the frame at the mirror causing it to explode into pieces and spread out across the floor like shrapnel from defective ammunition.

"Are you okay?" I repeated, hoping that this time I could muster some sort of response from her.

She gradually looked up, her eyes were dry and crusty, day-old tears had left indentations on her skin. She looked tired, she looked dissociated and all the rosiness that had been slowly returning had vanished once again into an unreachable abyss.

"She keeps looking at me" she breathed.

"Who?" I asked completely bewildered. There was no one else in the room.

"Her…" she pointed to the broken mirror. The shattered

mirror only revealed illusions of duplicate reflections of my own face. But she was convinced that there was someone else in the room. I looked over at the window, it was still tightly shut. I rubbed her arm gently and then proceeded to search the house. Having concluded that the house was safe and that there was no intruder, I went back into her room and knelt beside her. She looked petrified as if she'd seen a malicious spirit.

"It's okay. There's no one here" I reassured her.

I slowly lifted her by the arm and gently directed her away from the glass and out of the room looking back one more time at the destruction my frail mother managed to let out. That was the first-time one fragment of my mother ceased to exist.

The second time was more traumatic, something I could never forget. I was downstairs, reclined on the sofa. It was a quiet day, and I had nothing and nowhere to be. Meira was bathing upstairs, and my mother was asleep in her room. Or so I thought. Suddenly, I heard Meira scream at the top of her lungs. I sprang off the sofa and dashed up the stairs as quickly as I could.

The bathroom door was slightly ajar, and I called out her name, not wanting to disturb Meira as she bathed. I thought that perhaps she saw a mouse or an insect of some sort. But as I got closer, I noticed someone else was in the room with her.

I pushed the door open and instantly noticed the puddles of water all over the floor. The bathtub was partially full, and my mum was sat on the floor. Her sleeves had been rolled up, but they were damp, and she was leaning into the tub, holding Meira's head underwater. Meira was thrashing, gasping for air. Her face, her hair was soaking wet. I shouted, ran to my mother and pushed her with such force that she stumbled back and yelped out in distress. I frantically pulled Meira out of the tub and wrapped a towel around her. She was shaking, staring at me with wide eyes and panting for air.

"I was giving Meira a bath" mother smiled. "Why did you stop me?"

"A bath? She can bathe herself mum. What the hell were you doing?". I didn't mean for my tone to come across so rude, but I couldn't control myself. I couldn't believe what I saw.

"Of course. I was helping". She smiled again and then looked at Meira.

"Come on" she gestured, waving for her to come back to the bathtub. "You didn't finish your bath". "No mum. You tried to drown me!" she screamed, her body shivering viciously against mine.

I stared at her horrified, my mother was like a child, she giggled to herself and then turned serious almost instantly. I threw my body in between Meira and my mother when my mother suddenly stood up and took a step towards Meira.

"No mum" I spoke firmly, holding my hand up in front of her. "No".

"I said come here" she insisted, holding out her hands as she was trying to pick up a baby.

"Mum" I said as gently as I could, "why don't you go and rest?"

"When's your dad coming home?" she asked with a perplexed look on her face, turning her attention to me. "I don't remember when he said".

Meira and I gazed at each, completely stunned by what was happening. This wasn't normal behaviour, by any means. This changed everything. Mum needed help. Meira was no longer safe in the house. I was absolutely terrified at the thought of what would've happened if I wasn't at home.

"He'll be home soon" I smiled trying to suppress my fear.

"Liar!" she yelled. "He's dead".

"Okay mum…why don't you get some sleep okay?".
She nodded, stood up gently and shuffled out of the room. Meira moved back, her hands clutching my arms in protection.

"Make sure you give our dad some food when he comes home. And tell him I lost his baby. Tell him I'm not a mother anymore…" she mumbled as she left the room and slowly entered her room and shut the door.

I stood still, completely haunted by everything. She wasn't herself at all, and I had no idea what to do. I looked at Meira, her beautiful brown eyes looked lost and terrified. I squeezed her and took a deep breath, as deep as my lungs could go. There was an overwhelming burden on my shoulders and only I could carry it. I wanted for the first time to cry out loud, as far as the wind could carry it, but I had to be strong. I smiled at Meira and told her to go to her room. She was terrified, she didn't let me go but I assured her that I would be right outside.

To ease my pounding heartbeat, I sat on the edge of the bath that was still soaked with water. For a few minutes I recollected my thoughts. But they were jumbled and disorientated. I prayed that the world around me would stop spinning for one second. But it didn't. I couldn't stop thinking about it. My mother tried killing her daughter. My mother tried killing her daughter.

"Are you okay?" Sami asked as we walked to school the next day. I wanted to ask him about how he was doing, but I could still see traces of the wall he built, I didn't want to trespass.

"No…Something's wrong with my mother…"

We stayed silent for a minute as we crossed the gravel pathway onto the other side of the walkway. At this time of the morning, the paths were exceptionally busy. Cyclists would ride through the middle of these paths, and pedestrians would walk on the edges and so many times, cyclists would narrowly miss pedestrians as they went past. The ground was sandy, with a few pebbles that sometimes got in between my toes and made me wince in pain so I had learnt to start wearing trainers instead of slippers. The buildings were all made of stone, although some were built higher up than others. Laundry lines were attached across walls like spider webs and at times cyclists would have to be careful to avoid becoming twisted in them or worse, getting strangled.

Our town had many animals that would sneak in from the forests and the desert. Snakes were common, and for that reason we often avoided the back alleys because that's where there was an abundance of them. Cats, dogs, birds, and sometimes wild foxes would run across people's feet as they walked and they would get trampled on or kicked during the rush hour, usually between the hours of 7am and 9am. My father had bought me a bike a couple of years ago, but I used it for a week before I cycled it into a ditch and ruined the chain. I didn't mind it to be honest because it meant I could continue walking to school with Sami.

"I'm afraid" I finally admitted to Sami as we turned the corner. Although I had promised my mum never to tell anyone about Meira, Sami was the only one I did tell. But that was because I trusted him with my life.

"What do you mean?"

"She tried drowning Meira" I said abruptly. I could see his shock from the corner of my eyes. "She's been talking to herself, throwing things around the room. And Meira she is more insistent now, we must lock every door. After that incident she tried to get out of the house, and I managed to stop her just in time".

Sami looked down and I could see he was concerned about something.

"I'm sure it's nothing" he partially smiled. "Look…I'll be honest with you. You can't protect her for the rest of your life, it's impossible. One day, she'll be older and wiser, and she will realise you tried to protect her. As for your mum, I know she's grieving but it's not normal. What if you admitted her to Naghaar asylum?"

My eyes shot furiously up at him.

"No no" I disagreed frantically.

"I don't mean it like that" Sami reassured. "I just mean, maybe she needs a special institution so she can be helped. I'm not saying she's mad".

"What about Meira? Who will look after her whilst I'm at school?".

"The maids? Can't they?".

"Perhaps. But at night, when the maids go home, what if Meira escapes then? My mother's not a psychopath. The bloody council already referred her to the asylum before and I never replied to them".

"Hmmm" Sami replied gently. "Of course she's not mad. But if you need her to return to her normal self, she might need the help".

"Perhaps…" I mumbled.

The rest of the journey I thought about it. Maybe Sami was right. Maybe she needed the help, the kind of help I couldn't provide. At the end of the school day, I returned home, wrote the letter, and stamped it to be sent to Naghaar asylum. I placed it in my draw and closed it. I didn't even want to think about it. I felt heartless.

A meaningless vow

Talia

"Your husband is your priority. You need to make sure you keep him happy. Visit us only with his permission but don't visit us often. Make sure he is well fed and looked after. Make sure to keep him pleased. Always dress up for him and make yourself presentable".

I looked at my mum vacantly. Over the last few days, I had watched my mother morph into a stranger, who had more interest in the money and the wedding rather than trying to heal all the wounds on my knees from all the days I begged her to listen.

"Anything else?" I sarcastically asked.

"Yes" my mother continued. "I told Lucia's parents to not let her contact you again. Once you're married the only person you need is your husband. Is that clear?"

I sat up out of bed, my mind tried to frantically decipher her words.

"Am I getting married or being sent to prison?"

I threw the duvet off my body and jumped out of bed. "You got what you want didn't you? You're forcing me to marry a man who is almost twice my age! I'm getting married, aren't I? So why are you now asking me to isolate myself and sacrifice everything to keep him happy. What about me? Do I not matter?!"

She raised her eyebrows and her wrinkles imprinted deeper into her skin.

"She's my best friend mum. Please don't take away the one thing I have left!" I cried. "What about my letters? Did Lucia even receive them?".

"It's already been decided. Tamin has also expressed his

wish for you to stop studying. You will no longer attend school. You will stay home and look after him and give him children"

"I can't believe you" I whispered under my breath. It felt like she had ripped me away from everything I had ever known.

"You're an ungrateful child. We have brought you up in the best health and given you all the money in the world. Your birth mother would have never been able to give you that. It's not like you would've done anything with that education anyway".

My mum began to move around the room angrily, occasionally grumbling to herself and throwing her gaze over at me.

"You've never talked about her".

"Who?" she spat.

"My birth mum. Who was she? What happened to her?"

"Your birth mum was a whore; she was poor and gave

birth to you. I'm surprised she gave birth to such a beautiful baby seeing as she was ugly herself. And she gave you away to us because you were a burden. Like you're being a burden to me now!" she yelled.

"I'm sure she would've loved me more than you do" I cried.

"Pfff" she grumbled, puffing her cheeks in frustration. "I don't know where this is coming from. Thank God you're marrying, or I don't know what would've become of you". I could feel a knot at the pit of my windpipe, and the ropes of this knot had descended and wrapped my heart, squeezing all the life out of me.

"Tell me her name" I demanded.

"You don't need to know that" she replied angrily.

"And my real father?"

"Talia, that's enough!" she yelled pointing her finger at me.

"Quite frankly they are dead to me as they should be to you. Stop dwelling on the past and focus on your future.

"Now…" she took a deep breath and shook her head as if she was releasing the tension in her body. "I don't care what you want. Now go have a bath, clean yourself up and help with the decorations. And I've chosen out the dress you'll wear tomorrow. It'll be steamed and ready at 8am. Nela will be coming to get you ready".

She stormed out the room and slammed the door behind her.

I sat down on the bed for a moment. I filtered out any noise that penetrated my eardrums, afraid that any sound would break my quivering bones. After a few minutes, I stood up gingerly and made my way to the bathroom. I had lost the strength to speak and began to feel that I was better off 10 feet under. Then the thought hit me. Did the Pariah girls deserve such treatment? At that moment, I began to think about my own future maybe because my own future was a stone's throw away. I understood why women were kicked out and forced to live in the Pariah zone, it was because they had no choice. The Pariah girls had to choose between staying in a world where there would be no certainty if they woke up wanting to take their own life or choosing to live in a zone where they would feel like they were a part of something. Whether that was the friendships they built with other women or whether it was the simple pleasure of waking up and having a choice as to how they wanted to spend the rest of their day. The Pariah girls were not guilty.

They were powerless.

I caught a glimpse of myself in the mirror and noticed the outline of my bones protruding out of my hands. The last few days I had barely eaten and was bordering on the edge of keeping faith or losing the will to live. I was in a bottomless dark pit, consumed by the fear of marrying a man I didn't love but trying to keep myself afloat for the man that I did. A man that wanted nothing to do with me. I hadn't thought of my birth mum for a while but now that the reality of marrying sunk in, I wanted to know where I came from. I wanted to know whether it was just me that was cursed or whether it ran in my blood. A few moments later, my mum stormed back into the room and grabbed the steam iron from my cabinet.

"I don't understand mum" I murmured.

"What now?" she groaned, shooting her eyes up at me.

"Why you stopped loving me".

She sighed and then groaned loudly.

"You're delusional Talia. I still love you"

"You can't say you love someone and then let them die" I whispered.

"You won't die Talia! Pfff" she groaned. "So dramatic!"

"How would you know mum? You weren't around enough

recently to know me. I may look live alive, but I'm dead inside".

"Then maybe Tamin can revive you" she smiled. "Isn't that what love is supposed to be?"

Deep in my guts, I wanted to tell her that love wasn't meant to confine you, nor cage you, nor make you feel as if you owe that person something. But she would never understand. How could I force myself to love someone when they were a stranger to me? Although, I expected this one day, I just wished it wasn't real.

"You don't know anything about love" I muttered.

She swung her head around and folded her arms tightly.

"Maybe I don't…maybe you'll teach me then".

A change in my future

Kalei

Sami had barely left his house; he had stopped coming to school. Every time I visited him, he always made some excuse that he couldn't talk, and he shut the door in my face. After our walk to school, he had admitted everything that had been happening to him. Although I knew Sami's father had been hitting him, from the countless times I saw the bruises it wasn't the only thing his father did. I won't recall all the details; they were too disgusting to even think about. But his father had grown lonely after Sami's mother died and although he tried to quench that thirst with Pariah women, he was never satisfied enough.

Sami kept him satisfied.

That poor boy, seventeen years of age had to endure his father's abusive behaviour for eight years. Eight whole years that I never even knew about. And it shook me to the core. Sami always had a smile on his face, he was the one to always pull me out of the darkness. But my sadness seemed minute to the scale of his. At least I could escape my grief, his home was his grief. It's true what people say, the happiest people hide the darkest secrets. They are the ultimate masters of pretending. And it was now as if he was ashamed. As if he didn't want to face me because he knew that somebody knew his reality.

I spoke to the police, they said they would investigate, but I know they didn't bother. I filed several reports but just as the last one before, they ignored it. It seemed an abusive parent didn't warrant an arrest let alone a warning. I was angry, frustrated, I wanted to punish his father, I wanted to hurt him like he hurt Sami. But I had no power. Not yet anyway. It made me realise how important power was, in a world like this, power and wealth did in fact make a difference.

With the money I would get after the pledge which would be around 3000 garoles, I could take Sami away from all the pain he was enduring. I could buy him a home away from his father. I could help him find some solace. But for now, I had to hold on and watch corruption poison the town, and all I could do was allow the last remaining healthy parts of this town's body to die whilst I watched.

It was a cold foggy morning, yet the sun was still bright. The sky was a mixture of whites and blues, and the clouds looked as thick as a cigar's smoke trapped in a glass jar. I was sat out in the garden, contemplating, thinking, preparing. Any day now Talia would be a part of the seeking ceremony. Any day now she would belong to someone else but me. I desperately missed her, her comfort and her smile. I often thought of that day in the meadow, I thought of the way she made me feel, and the way her skin felt against mine. It was hard enough trying to amputate the fibre that kept her attached to me, but it was harder to extinguish the fire that still burnt in my soul for her.

I prayed that her husband would be good to her. I prayed that he knew how much she felt at ease when fresh rainwater hit the warm concrete and that smell made her want to run out and stay in the open air and get soaked to the skin. I hoped he knew how much she loved cinnamon and that the smell of vanilla in her hair had the power to warm the body like an isolated cabin fireplace in a blizzard. But most of all, I wished she would fall in love with him, just so she would forget how I broke her heart.

"Kalei"

I looked behind me to see my mother standing on the front doorstep. She trudged slowly along the cobbled pathway, holding her lower back.

"Are you okay mother?"

She groaned as she sat down on the floor beside me. She seemed normal today.

"I'm okay. I'm just getting old" she chuckled. Hearing even a faint laugh in her voice warmed me up. She didn't know it, but she held the home together, she held me together.

"Still so beautiful though" I smiled. "Come on. You shouldn't be sat on the ground". As I leaned forward to help her up, she paused a little and then looked at me sombrely.

"Kalei…I won't live forever…"

"Mum…"

"No" she put her hand up to stop me talking. "We may see our parents as immortal but they're not. You forget I'm getting older too"

"Mum, you don't…I don't know why you're saying this…"

"Because…" she placed her hand on my cheek, and I squeezed my eyes shut to embrace her touch. One that I hadn't felt in a while.

"I want you to learn to be independent. Although I will always be with you, I won't always be on earth. I want you to be strong. Lead by example and Meira will follow"

"I feel like we corrupted her" I admitted quietly. "Nothing is the same between us".

She withdrew her hand and placed it on her lap.

"I know. Maybe not now, but one day she will truly appreciate you"

"I hope so. I'm just scared that maybe all those years of keeping her inside might turn her into a monster? What if her desire to break out of her cage only turns her into a devil, whilst I'm trying to persuade her that her cage is the safest place to be?".

"I am sure that with you to guide her she will be safe. I believe in you…It's not long until you take your pledge".
She looked at me knowing that I was surprised that she finally brought the topic up

"Take the money and take Meira away from here"

"What?" I stared at her. "What do you mean?"

"I don't want you to be a council member. All you'll end up becoming is a shadow of a man. Someone who will never have enough time for his family. Your grandfather was like that. He cared more about his fame and wealth than he did for your dad".

"But you've always said…" I was disorientated and taken aback with what she said. "I've always been prepared to take the pledge when I turned eighteen".

"I know Kalei. I know what I'm saying is shocking. Please, I beg you. Take the allowance money you're given on the pledge day and leave Naghaar. Take Meira and go and live your life!".

I began to cry. It felt as if someone lifted the heaviest boulder off my shoulders. All my life I prepared for this and now I was finally given the permission to discard it. My mother would not resent me. She wouldn't curse me for ruining everything. I was allowed to leave.

"But mum, I would become a defector"

"By the time they figure that out, I hope you'll be long gone!" she laughed.

"Are you sure mum? Everything will change if I do that"

"I know I have lost my mind recently, but you don't think I can see when my son is burdened? I know you never wanted to be a member. After losing your father I realised that he never spent time with you. Yes, I loved him, but I barely saw him. I never want that for you. I want you to come home to a happy wife, who you'll sit down and have dinner with. And you'll be able to have conversations with your children because to them you are always present. Not absent. That's what life is supposed to be like…"

"I'm going to take you too mum. One day, we will find our way out of here".

She didn't reply. She leaned her head on my shoulder and for the next few minutes we sat on the ground listening to the birds' chirp and feeling the breeze caress our skin.

Suddenly, I shot my head up.

"Kalei, what's wrong?".

I stood up, my heart began to race.

"Kalei?" my mother asked, concerned about me.

"I need to go!" I beamed.

"Where?"

Before I could answer her, I was already running out of the garden and down the street. I ran as fast as my legs could take me.

I was going to do it.

I was going to tell Talia that I would marry her. As soon as I took the pledge, as soon as I got my allowance money, I would take my family, perhaps Sami too, and take Talia away from here. I was going to do it.

The 10th of January

Talia

The 10th of January was my wedding day. Nela walked in early that morning and in her plump, large hands she carried a silk white dress and threw it onto the foot of the bed. It was an ivory colour, with gold threads embroidered in the shape of white roses. Its' neckline was high and narrow, and its' sleeves were contrastingly large and puffy. I got out of bed groggily and held it up to inspect it. I watched as the lace of the skirt fell to the ground and the early dawn sun rays shone its golden colours through it. This was *my* wedding dress. I couldn't comprehend the idea that this was the dress that I would wear when shaking hands with my fate.

It felt as if I was trapped in the loop of a never-ending coma and the only thing, I did have control of was my own heartbeat, and even that was going too fast for my own comfort.

Nela was a short scrawny woman, with silver rimmed glasses and a large mole underneath her left eye. She was the town's only makeup artist, every woman in Naghaar booked Nela for special occasions, but I had never been fond of makeup, not heavy makeup anyway. I watched as Nela took out a tattered leather bag and pulled out a palette of bright colours.

"Sit down" she ordered in a deep voice.

At 7.43am I watched as the darkness under my eyes disappeared and to replace me was a complying and cheerful body double. This body double was beautifully deceptive to the negligent eye. The dress that clung onto her skin elevated her frail frame and made her appear taller than she was. Her long thick black hair had been pinned up behind her head, and only a few strands fell to structure her sunken cheeks. Her lips were stained with a bright red colour that had also been blended on the tip of her narrow nose and on her eyelids. An intense crimson shade had been spread onto her cheekbones, but the colour disappeared under her pale skin. And as every second passed, I watched this clone rip away every layer of blissful memories I had of the innocent and plain little girl I used to be.

"You're done" Nela muttered quietly.

I blinked slowly and there I was.

A bride.

As a young girl, I had dreams sketched messily on scraps of papers of this very day. These drawings were of a happy woman, smiling ear to ear with her hands clasped with her beloved betrothed. That should've been Kalei I thought...

If only I could go back and tell that little girl that her

dreams would never come true. I couldn't control myself, and I burst out in tears that began to forge a river through the cosmetic veil freshly painted on my skin.

"Ay ay" Nela muttered. "You messed it up"
I sat there and watched Nela frantically dip her fingers in colours and repaint my face.

At that moment my mum had walked in and asked Nela why I was not ready. Nela complained that my tears ruined her work and that she was running late for her next booking. For the next 20 minutes, whilst Nela recreated the previous look, my mother lectured me about how I wasted time, money and how I needed to put on an agreeable opaque mask that no one could see through.
"This wedding is happening whether you like it or not. Cry your way out of it and Nela will just keep re-doing it. Today you will become Tamin's wife".

By the time Nela was done, I watched as the body double seized the girl's reflection once more and the old me faded before my eyes. I was untouched, ceramic like with bright red cheeks and glossy skin. The paleness of my skin was a stark contrast to my dark black hair that was pinned back into a beautiful thick updo, and this face was indeed a face of a woman that resembled…a China doll.

A few minutes later, my mother handed me a bouquet of flowers. They were a mixture of rues and dark green vines. At this point, I was completely numb. It was hard to explain. Almost as if I was detached from my body. My body was here on earth, its' beautiful visage masking the unbearable pain I had inside. In another realm, my soul had fallen into the deepest depths of hell, burning, and pounding in stillness within its' flames. There was nothing else I could do. The doors of my bedroom opened and there stood my dad. He looked at me, his face completely emotionless. He was wearing his council attire, and my stomach sank in repulsion.

"Hurry up" he muttered. "Everyone's waiting".

As I walked down the hallway of my home, women were scattered around, whispering, and smiling as I passed by. Some congratulated me, some smiled, and others were in complete surprise at my changed appearance. My mother followed closely behind soaking in all the words of affirmation as if she was the one taking her vows. I could feel my mother's joy radiate around my empty shell. My legs were shaking intensely as I began to make my way down the stairs. The weight of my body felt intolerable that I was sure I would collapse and snap into two. But I thought that perhaps that wouldn't be a bad thing. Maybe if threw my body down the stairs it would be the perfect escape. But what if I permanently damaged myself instead? I would only be condemning myself to the Pariah zone. But what if

I died? No, that was too easy. I would perjure myself and risk returning as a ghost, one that would linger in between the folds of time, begging to find a permanent place away from the house that used to be my home.

Even in my grave they would not leave me alone. Even in darkness they would find a way to dig me out and reclaim my remains to use for their own benefit.

The house was alive with colours of all shades and flowers of the most beautiful silhouettes and distinctiveness. The bustle that travelled through the rooms made it seem as if the house was born from the petals of tranquillity. As if that moment was a dream that had finally come true for everyone. It was all a lie. There in the living room, underneath the white canopy he stood.

My soon to be husband.

His thin black hair had been brushed back and bonded to

his greasy forehead. He had cleaned up, his scruffy ash coloured beard had been brushed down, and his shirt could barely stretch enough to cover up his flabby belly. I was ushered to stand in front of him, and he inspected my whole body as if he was proud that he finally claimed his prize.

After a moment, the men, and women around, most of whom I had only ever seen when passing through the market had gathered too as if they were close acquaintances. They quietened down and the silence in the air intensified the echo of my thoughts. I didn't look up. I couldn't look up. As I stared down at my white shoes, from the corner of my eye I saw another man take his place between us. I quickly darted my gaze up to see my father standing before me.

"Thank you all for attending" he spoke. "We are here to witness the marriage of Tamin Shodar with my daughter, Talia Arman".

He looked stern, not the face of a man who had to give away his only daughter. At what point did he stop loving me? There were endless hours, days, months and years when I tried to get him to see me. Not just to see me but to know me. But he never did. Whilst he read out the vows, I drifted into the only peaceful place in my mind that I could find. The meadow. And there in the meadow stood Kalei, waiting for me, and I could run towards him, and feel and breathe. I could just breathe.

A few minutes later I was brought back to reality at the sight of a large hand being held out in front of me. I looked up to find Tamin waiting for me to take it. I was considering taking the cake knife and slicing it through his hand or distracting everyone, throwing myself out the window and running across the desert pan towards the trees. But I had nothing that could sustain me out there. I was insistent that only a man could make a woman whole, and so, without Tamin, I would be nothing.

Within those brief seconds, it felt as if the whole world was frozen around me and only my heart was moving, trying to beat while my body was dying, but it was still a sign to me that I was alive. And that counted for something. I slowly placed my hand in Tamin's, the first time I had touched a man's hand other than Kalei's. His skin was coarse and dry, not like Kalei's, and Tamin squeezed it hard as if he could read the thoughts I had.

"You are now man and wife" my father said. "Congratulations".

It was a surreal moment. Everyone applauding as you drowned. And my mother, who brought me up, watched me take my first steps and fed and clothed me…how could she smile knowing her daughter was no longer hers? I was another man's property. And we all know what happens with property.

It becomes furnished, renovated, painted with colours and eventually someone lives in that property and owns it. The walls reflect the habits of the occupier, the legs of the furniture carry their weight and for how ever many years that property remains in his hands until one day he decides it is no longer functional and puts it up for sale. And with the sale goes every memory lived there.

To certain occupiers the memories of that property stay with him forever, but to others the memories mean nothing as long as he has cash in his hand. Tamin leaned over to me, and I could smell the desperation and greed like a permanent stench that clung to him.

"You are now mine" he whispered.

As we walked out, he grabbed my hand and squeezed it in his sweaty palms. The front door opened, and everyone followed us out as we walked down the garden pathway towards the gate. They threw petals on us, petals that stuck to my hair.

It was a rainfall of colour on a dark day.

And as Tamin laughed and smiled and greeted everyone, in the far distance I saw a figure gazing at me. I narrowed my eyes because I thought I was imagining. I thought I was seeing things. But no. There Kalei stood, with his hands dug deep in his pockets. Tears rolled down his face.

I saw Kalei that day. On my wedding day, I saw him watch me, the same man I wanted to so desperately marry. But instead, my hand was in another's, and all I could do was glare at him and somehow through my eyes tell him that I was never going to forgive him. I was never going to forgive him because he was supposed to help me forget him.

Why then did he come here?

Kalei

I looked everywhere for her. I checked her home, no one was there. I checked the Patlin, the markets, the council chambers. I tried rattling the iron gates of the school too, but nobody was there. And it was then I thought I would run by her house once again. But this time I would knock on her door. I would ask her parents where she was. I didn't care about how they would react seeing me standing in their doorway, I just needed to see her.

The moment I turned into her street, the silence that I had seen just a few minutes before had disappeared. Her front door had opened, and a cascade of men and women flooded out. They were throwing petals and within the large crowd I noticed a large man holding her hand.

She wore a white dress, the most beautiful dress I had ever seen. Her hair was majestic, the way it framed her face was like that of an angel's and I couldn't help but wonder what a terrible mistake I had made. She walked with no conviction, but the beauty on her face was a perfect mask to her dejected heart. As I watched from afar, she looked up at me and I felt the breath leave me. It was as if we were the only ones that existed at that moment. I began to cry. My heart stopped beating.

It was then that I realised, she got married…
I was too late…

Talia

The rest of the evening Tamin never let go of my hand. I could barely eat in the fear I would throw up. I couldn't stop thinking about Kalei. Seeing him just a few hours before, why was he here? Why did he have to torture me like this? During that evening's celebrations women gave me gifts that filled the table, and once that table was full, they began to give it in my hand. I had blankets, baskets of food, flowers that could cover the whole of Asia and Africa combined and masses of baby clothes surrounding my chair.

"I'm sure your mother told you" Tamin mumbled as he took a bite out of a chicken leg. "That you won't be going to school anymore…"

I didn't look up at him, I just stared down at the plate of food, nudging it with the end of my fork.

"I don't think girls need to be educated" he continued. "What's the use of it? That's what men are for. Your only job is to give me healthy boys. That's all I want. As long as you do that, you'll be happy".

He gnawed at the last bits of chicken and sucked the bone; he threw the bone onto the plate and wiped his fingers on the napkin. He then turned to me and gritted through his teeth.

"Look at me when I speak to you".

I took a deep breath and turned to look at him. He had crumbs all over his beard and his forehead was glistening with sweat.

"You are beautiful you know" he smiled vilely. "I paid a lot for you, you understand doll?".

He turned back to his food and continued to wolf it down. I dropped my fork, sat back into my chair, and watched everyone dance, drink and eat. My heart was breaking on the day it was meant to feel whole.

Am I a machine or a human?

Talia

"Are you getting into bed?" Tamin asked from behind me. His voice made me jump; I had completely forgotten he was there. I was too busy lost in my thoughts, staring out the window somehow hoping Kalei would turn up again. I told myself I hated him, that I would never forgive him, but who was I kidding? I couldn't ever hate him, and I hated myself for that.

"I'm not tired" I replied quietly.

"You can't refuse. Get here" he instructed.

I slowly walked over and sat on the edge of the bed. "Your father sent me a letter. He asked if you were doing well".

I didn't reply.

"I told him you were staying home now. No school. I also told him that if you didn't give me a healthy boy in the next three months, I would send you to the Pariah zone. You understand?"

"I…that's not in my control" I whispered.

"What?" he gritted. "What's your purpose then?"

"I…I don't know what my purpose is".

"Your purpose is what I tell you it is. You have three months doll, or you have no use for me".

The events of that night were too much for me to bear. He threw his body onto me that night, I could never forget the pain. How he flung himself on me, crushing my ribs under his intolerable weight. How every single sharp breath I took, I could feel a bone shatter and splinter and pierce through my skin. As each agonising second passed, I felt every sap of goodness leave me, I felt betrayed, the type of betrayal that etched deep into my core, leaving me gasping for air in a tumultuous current. It didn't make sense. My mother always told me tat the place between my legs was a sacred place. So why then, was this devil allowed to claim it?

I didn't know how I was supposed to feel or what to think. I didn't know whether I should've kept still or screamed till my lungs burst and let them paint the walls of this dark room.

I prayed to God for him to take my soul because I was afraid that I would have no soul left after this. I would rather have no soul that a broken one. And then, I felt an intense pain scorching the inside of my thighs and I grit the sheets and clenched my jaw so tight I was sure I heard a crack in the crown of my lower tooth. Once he was done, he turned over and went to sleep whilst I closed my eyes and wiped the tears with the back of my hand. There was once a time I wanted to become a woman but now I missed the shelter of girlhood. I would now be caught in the torrential rain every single waking day because I no longer had a safe space. I no longer had a land that was unclaimed. I painfully got out of bed, blood on the bedsheets, blood on my thighs and I bathed that night.

Whilst sat in the tub, I cried quietly to myself, it had to be so quiet so that Tamin wouldn't hear, but I knew my lungs still wanted to burst. I felt violated, I felt the body that I made memories in, found happiness in, were all taken away by a man's touch. In all the books I read, a man's love had the power to move the earth, but this love buried me in it. I watched as the tap continued to flow and the water rose past my ankles, up to my hips, to my chest and within it swirls of red floated around. I wanted to drift off into an infinite slumber and I had no care if this blood-tinged water took me. I was drowning in my hurt and my anxieties in the one place I should've felt complete. My home. But it wasn't my home, it was a house. One where Tamin dictated everything, one where I couldn't say or do anything without his permission. I was a puppet on strings, being manipulated by his hands.

In the darkness I wrapped my arms around my body, trying to imagine what embrace felt like, trying to imagine what Kalei's love used to feel like. I looked at my body, how disgusting I felt in my skin, water was not enough to cleanse me. I began to scrub my body with a thick coarse sponge in the hope that I would cleanse myself of him. My skin burned, turned red and was excruciatingly sore to the touch and that was when I was content that I was clean enough. "Please god" I wept under my breath. "Give me strength to live another day".

And I turned the water off just as it touched my lips and almost drowned me.

But this nightmare continued almost every single night, and every single night I imagined ways in which I could stop myself breathing, ways in which I could leave the temporary world. But only one thought stopped me. Him. It became a habit, and habit became a sacrament. Every night I turned off the dials of my heart, drifted into another world and allowed Tamin to believe I saw him as my world.

Overtime, the pain became bearable. Over time, the water level that I bathed in descended. From wanting to drown myself to slowly telling myself that this was a temporary affliction that I would have to endure. It was ironic. Tamin had a younger sister just a little older than me. I had never met her, only heard of her existence when Tamin briefly mentioned that she escaped to the city with a lover. I was sure that Tamin saw pieces of her in me that he wanted to control because he failed to control her. I would love to meet her one day and praise her for escaping the clutches of her brother, a monster not a man, a devil unshackled from hell.

A brewing war

Kalei

A body was found in the woods. This wasn't like the other bodies, no, this was a member of the council. Late at night the handlers had been patrolling the forest when they came across what seemed like a sack of wheat. Upon closer inspection, it was found to be the body of Ure Derin, a member of the Naghaar council. When news spread of this discovery, the council had organised an emergency meeting. There were fears, extreme fears that hadn't been felt in a while and they began to spread around town like wildfire. Naghaari's began to lock their doors at night, they began to stop leaving their homes after nightfall and Makni Armis had ordered more handlers to be put on duty at night.

It was rumoured that the Pariah's had once again began to kill. Ure Derin was found with an axe lodged in his upper stomach. A most brutal death by its nature. The question then arose, why was Ure in the forest at night? If he was in the forest after leaving the Pariah zone, why wasn't he accompanied by a handler? And if all these answers had been found, then why now, after so many years did the Pariah's, so submissive, so obedient, decide to rebel again? It was a thought that terrified the council.

I had been summoned to the chambers late that night, still half asleep, a knock had come at my door urging me to meet Makni Armis immediately. Upon arrival, Makni Armis gleamed at me, the dark circles under his eyes signalled to me he hadn't slept that night.

"Kalei, come" he gestured to me.

I sat down in front of him. He watched for a few seconds, with his hands in his laps and his legs awkwardly crossed over.

"I'm sure you've heard about Ure" he began, stroking his coarse white beard with his wrinkly hands.

I nodded.

"As you know the war between the Pariah's and Naghaari's has been going on for as long as any of us can remember. Your grandfather founded the system in order to try and bring some sort of order. But it seems the Pariah's, after so many years of *almost* submitting to our will, are attacking again. This is not like the times we've found bodies randomly in the woods. This was a council member. This has never happened before".

I nodded again, not quite sure how to reply.

"I called you here because I need to push forward your pledge date".

"What do you mean?"

"We need all the manpower we can get Kalei. The quicker you become a member, the quicker you can get trained in weapons use and the quicker we can have an extra helping hand".

"But Makni Armis, I…supreme leader…I'm not yet eighteen".

"I know that" he answered strongly.

"But…"

I wasn't ready. Not yet anyway. I had a few more weeks to enjoy what I had of my freedom. I felt as if it was being taken away too quickly.

"My mother…she's not well as you know. And…"

"We'll look after your mother" he answered putting his hand up in front of his face. "We will ensure she gets the best treatment".

"With all due respect, I don't want her to go to the asylum. I feel I can look after her more than anyone else can".

"This is a weakness boy!" he suddenly spat. "This is what the women in our family do. They pull you in, they use your goodness to keep you attached to them!".

He sighed loudly and then groaned in frustration.

"You will take your pledge this Sunday" he ordered. "That is an order".

"I'm sorry" I gulped. "I can't…".

I stood up, my legs were shaking under my weight. "My duty comes to my mother first. I will take the pledge, happily, when the time comes. But for now, she needs me…"

After I left the chamber that night, I felt completely numb. I was prepared to join the council in my head, but I wanted to join the council when I turned eighteen. Not now. It wasn't meant to happen now. I thought of what my mother said. *Take the money. Leave Naghaar.* Maybe I could've taken the pledge this Sunday, maybe I could've taken the money and left but my mother would not be able to handle the journey. She could barely walk in the house without somehow destroying something in her path. It was the right decision I told myself. No matter how angry Makni Armis looked, he would forgive me. I'm sure I wasn't the first to reject his order.

It was ominously dark outside and only one streetlamp lit the floor of my bedroom. I had been tossing and turning all night, waiting for the sunlight to creep in so I could talk to my mother about her treatment. I was excited about the prospect of finally getting my mother back to her old self.
After long silent moments a knock came at the door, I lifted my head to find my mother standing there. She was

smiling, the kind of smile that could light up the room.

"Why aren't you asleep?" I asked her across the room.

"I wasn't tired".

"Mum, what's wrong?".

"Nothing" she shook her head.

"Mum..." I bit my lip and then spoke. "I wanted to speak to you about this in the morning, but...I might as well tell you now..."

Gingerly she made her way to my bed and sat near my feet. She smiled at me and waited for me to speak. I sat up and shuffled in my seat.

"Mum...I'm going to get you better. I will be with you every step of the way. I promise. I won't leave you in the asylum. We're going to go there together and come back together. You'll be better by the time I take the pledge. And then we can leave Naghaar".

"You think I'm crazy, don't you?" her voice had grown more bitter and resentful in its tone.

"Why would you say that?" I asked taken aback by her voice.

"Asylum huh?" she mumbled. "That's what you think of me?!". She began to yell, and my heart had dropped into my stomach. I never meant to hurt her feelings, I just wanted to help her.

"No mum. I promise I didn't mean it like that….I just want to support you".

"No…" she paused. "You were supposed to just listen…"

"Listen to what?".

"I'm not living in an asylum" she huffed. "No way! I'm not mental Kalei!".

I threw the duvet off the bed and leaned in aggressively to hug her. I cradled her into my arms, she didn't melt into my affection like she used to do, she just began to cry into my shirt, wailing and sobbing uncontrollably.

"I don't know what's wrong with me Kal! I'm so lost! I don't love Meira; in fact, I'll admit I hate being her mother.

I miss your father terribly and I have no purpose in my life!" she muffled into my chest.

"How can you say you don't love Meira?!" I asked, pushing her head up so I could look her in the eyes. "She's your child!".

"You won't understand. You'll never understand. I'm trying. I tried…I…." she took a long breath. "…I'll be back…"

"Where are you going?"

"Don't worry" she smiled, wiping away her tears on her sleeve. "I'm okay. I'm just going to sit in the garden".

"It's past dark. I don't think you should" I shook my head.

"No Kal. I…I need to escape"

"But mum, it's no longer safe to be out after nightfall!"

"I'll be okay Kalei…I won't leave the garden".

Before I could ask her any further questions, she leaned in, kissed me on the cheek and walked out the room.

I considered going after her, but I thought that perhaps it was best to leave her. She needed the space, and she needed the time. There was so much she was going through under the surface of her painted happiness, I needed to let her breathe. Since that day that she tried to drown Meira, I had stayed home more often. I very rarely stepped outside in the fear it would happen again. Thankfully it didn't. But if there was any chance that my mother could heal somehow, I would take it.

It was early morning by the time I opened my eyes. The sky was a beautiful fusion of ambers and coppers, and every bird in the sky had come out singing their songs on the tallest treetops. Only a few Naghaari men were out on the street, sipping tea and talking about the day ahead. I got myself out of bed, I wasn't usually awake so early, but I wanted to see how my mother was doing. After last night's conversation I wanted to make sure that she was okay, and I was praying that she felt much better.

The floorboards creaked with every step as I made my way down the hallway, slowly pushing the door open, I found my mother's bed unslept in. I then quickly but quietly darted into Meira's room; she was fast asleep. I made my way over to her, leaned in and gave her a delicate kiss. She mumbled to herself quietly then turned over and fell back into a deep sleep. I made my way down the stairs, looking in every room and calling out for mum. There was no reply. She must've gone to the markets I thought.

After a few hours passed, Meira had awoken, and I could hear her footsteps travel between the bathroom and her room. She slowly staggered downstairs, yawning and rubbing her eyes.

"Where's mum?" she asked drowsily.

"I'm not sure" I replied.

"Did she mention anything about going out to you?"

She shook her head.

"Listen Meira…" I turned my body to her. But before I could carry on talking, she walked into the kitchen and lit the match to the fire. I followed her in. She began to boil some water, busying herself and clanging pots and pans so that I had to raise my voice over the noise.

"There's something I need to tell you. A lot of things are going to change. Did you hear about Ure Derin?"

She glanced over at me but didn't say a word.

"Well…"

"Apparently more bodies have been found…I read it in the newspaper…" she finally said. "In the woods. The handlers killed some Pariah's last night that were trespassing during the night. Apparently, they killed Ure".

"Oh, I didn't know. Anyway, I was saying. I'm taking the pledge this Sunday".

"What?" Meira suddenly dropped the pans and turned her body sharply towards me. Her eyebrows furrowed deeply into her skin.

"Before you say anything…I'm taking the money. That's all".

"What do you mean?"

"Mum encouraged me too. But I'm going to take the pledge and take the pledge money they give me. We're leaving Naghaar".

Meira's eyes lit up like a crackling fireplace. I put my hand on her shoulder, praying she didn't withdraw under my touch. To my relief, she didn't and instead she smiled.

"When? Where? Wait, but you're not eighteen?" a deeper light ignited behind her eyes.

"Because of all the killings recently, Makni Armis wants me to become a part of the council as soon as possible. And so, I decided, I don't want to be a member. I want nothing to do with it. If I become a member, your life will become more impossible than it is right now. I can't do it. And so, we'll go anywhere away from here. Anywhere where your gender, your worth is never judged."

"Is there such a place we can go?"

"We will find it Meira. Together"

"You swear? This is not a joke, right?"

"No" I reassured her. "I promise".

She stepped towards me and wrapped her arms around my torso. I leaned my chin on the top of her head and closed my eyes. It was a moment that I waited so long for, and it was moment that I wished could last forever.

"Kalei…" she breathed. "I'm so excited…"

We both smiled at each other, lost in our hopes for the future.

"I'm going to the market to see if I can find mum, okay?"

She nodded and then smiled. I never realised just how

much I missed seeing the beautiful gap in her lips and the way it revealed her perfect pink gums. I grabbed my jacket, slipped on my boots and dashed out the front door.

I bolted down the street and within a few minutes I was at Sami's front door. I pounded on it; I knew that I would probably be waking Sami up, but I had no choice. He was the only one that could help me. After what felt like slow agonizing minutes, he opened the door. Rubbing his eyes, he looked at me in confusion.

"Kal?" he yawned.

"Sami I'm so sorry to have woken you but could you help me find my mother? She's been gone for hours, and she's not returned. Can you help me look for her?"

Sami quickly threw on his jacket and followed me.

"So, she's definitely not at home?"

"No. She's not home"

"Where could she have gone?"

As we walked briskly through the markets, I searched every face. Cloaked women, women with long mops of hair, older women, but no one that resembled my mother. I was truly panicking now.

"Let's do this" Sami stopped in his tracks. He looked in both directions down the path.

"I'll go to the school, and you go to the butcher's street. Maybe she's there".

"Kalei!". Just then a handler appeared around the corner, rushing towards me, panting and out of breath. Sweat dripped from his forehead as if he ran for miles endlessly.

"Mr Roman, your mother!".

"What about her?" I asked, my heart in my throat and panic seeping into my veins.

"Follow me" he urged.

I followed the handler, with Sami close behind and all three of us ran as fast as we could. As fast as my legs could thrust me. My heart raced, my blood pumped, and the wind brushed past my ears as if to say *slow down*. I cut corners, jumped over fallen fruit baskets and let my heart lead me to the woman who gave me half of it

Barren

Talia

I was still barren. At least that's what Tamin always said. And life as I knew had changed for the worse.

It was a crisp and cold Thursday morning, and the leaves that were once dry and wilted had transformed into the most beautiful shade of coppers and greens in preparation for springtime. The streets were deathly quiet with only the faint sound of crunching as neighbours walked into their homes, closed their doors, and prepared food for the day ahead. I had always favoured serenity over noise and these preferences were also scrupulously upheld by my new neighbours.

My new home was much smaller than I was used to. With only four bedrooms, it felt cramped to me, and I hated the moss green colour that Tamin had painted the walls. Our neighbours were an old couple, married for 63 years but they very rarely left the house since I moved here. I could smell fresh bread baking on their stove almost every day and from time to time I would peer out the window to see the old woman with an array of delicious baked goods dispersed across her bright yellow tablecloth. The neighbours to my right were a small family, consisting of 2 parents and 2 young children. They would always have company around and great company it would seem by the sounds of cheering and laughter through the thin veneer of paint in my living room wall.

The street I lived on was not too far from my parent's house, and although it looked very similar in appearance, with the same cobbled footpath leading to the brown wooden garden gate, the bright white alley walls felt different here. Here, I felt alone and isolated. I was missing Lucia terribly, and I had a strong urge to sneak out, go to her house and ask her how she had been. But Tamin had me under surveillance. He had asked me a million questions whenever I returned home from the markets and although I had managed to convince him, he had begun to follow me around.

I even missed my parents. It was remarkable considering, they were the ones to force me to marry him. But when I thought about it, I probably didn't miss them, but I missed the familiarity of being around them. I had stopped going to school, but I kept my mind alive through excessive reading and writing. I didn't write anything in particular, just random thoughts that I would later burn in case Tamin ever came across them. I passed my days by cooking, cleaning, and doing the laundry. It would take me hours just to scrub Tamin's clothes on the washboard because he had always dirtied it with the way he ate. Very rarely, he would compliment me or show me affection, but I had already braced myself to accept that this was perhaps how the rest of our marriage would be.

Soon after our wedding, Tamin had fired the help because according to him I would never learn how to be a wife. Tamin was fairly rich, he still went to work at the local factory that specialised in cycles and household items, but the majority of his income had been given to him by his deceased father. But I was certain that he only went to work because he would get food brought to him on silver platters and he would brag to me how the workers there worshipped him like he was the Adonis of the Asian world. From time to time, I would look out from my window, and watch the Pariah's in the far-off distance. A young woman, probably around my age was sat cross legged on the floor, she was fidgeting with the wire in the fence, she looked lost in her thoughts. Another woman, a little older had a baby in her arms. I sighed to myself, grateful that although I was extremely unhappy at least I was safe, warm, and still had my dignity intact.

After Ure's death, not many Pariah's trespassed into Naghaar. It was too risky for them. Makni Armis still allowed Pariah's to work in Naghaar but I was sure it was to monitor them closely more than anything. Maybe he had hoped to overhear their conversations that might've somehow informed the council about the Pariah's future attack plans. Things these days were all just maybes. No one was sure of anything. More often I started seeing Naghaari's throw food at the Pariah's, spit at them, curse them. In one case, a Naghaari man threw his urine on a Pariah who was doing her job. I was disgusted and shocked because I always knew the situation in town was volatile, but the disparity just felt too close to home.

Just a few days before I told Tamin that I thought I was expecting and that was the first time he hugged me with genuine affection. If I was carrying a life, I didn't know how to feel about it because any memory of that moment of conception traumatised me. How could something so beautiful be created by a moment so painful?
Tamin had recently spent all his time stuck to the sofa, and he had been eating more than his weight in prunes and biscuits that within the past week he had looked much larger

than before. The house remained shrouded in deafening silence, there was not much to talk about between us. The most he would ask is whether his 'boy' was okay, to which I would reply that he was. Any other answer would trigger him and out of nowhere he would criticise, swear and curse me that I shrank like a little child and refused to look in the mirror for days. After all, how could I be useful, how could I be loved if I didn't remain beautiful to him?

A reputation to protect

Kalei

We were now racing through the trees, deep in Naghaar forest. I brushed past branches, tripped over tree trunks that had spread their legs across the forest floor, forgot to focus on my breathing that the sky began to whirl, pricked my fingers on nettles, submerged my boots in muddy water, and ran as fast as I could. The sun had now come out at the highest peak and trickled in through the gaps in the forest canopy. I felt as if I had failed as a son. Here I was running through the forest, chasing shadows, chasing voices that sounded like hers. I saw her face in shapes of trees and felt fingers up my legs as if she was tugging at them from below.

I had no idea how vast the forest was, but I closely followed the handler who was twisting and turning in every direction. It felt like everything had changed. As a brother and as a son, I was torn between the duties ordained by God. The most important girls in my life had to suffer and it was all a system that traced back through my blood, it was my lineage that had ruined the upcoming generation, my past damaged the future. There was no going back to the life we had. It was a cruel twist of fate. That is what scared me about life, the way it can change so suddenly, how can one truly be content with life when everything you know can suddenly be taken away? All I could think about was how life is precarious and unpredictable, as was death, and although there is no escape from the morbid reality of life, death finds a way to claim us one way or another.

As I continued to jump, run, speed I thought about Meira. There had not been a single day where she would be left alone. She lived her life in our company, and she would live every coming hour in mine too. We finally stopped in our tracks, I took in large gulps of air, the lower right area of my abdomen was now stinging and sending sharp aches through my body every time I inhaled. Ahead of us was a large pond, with several small streams branching from it. Two small birds were sat on the still water, they were identical in appearance. One of them used its black needle like beak, dipped it into the water and threw its head back to swallow, its bright red eyes blinking at me. There was only one path that ran near the pond, although the path wasn't clearly marked, low hanging branches partially blocked the route, rocks were strewn everywhere and small mine like holes punctured the soft brown surface. There was nothing else I could see, everywhere was just greens and browns, some trees arched over and blocked some sunlight that only patches of the soil were brightened with the value that daylight gifted. The trees reached so high that heaven must've had its leaves as its terrain. I looked over at the handler who nodded as to say this way, and we followed the path, I prayed under my breath that it led somewhere. That it led to her, and that it led to her alive and well. Why would she be so deep in the forest? For what possible reason?

"You've not said a word" I asked the handler as we made our way down the path. We had stopped running now, only walking briskly so we could catch our breath.
"You need to see for yourself" said the handler, avoiding

eye contact with me. After what felt like an hour, the river beside us had finally stopped and it was now just a large pond, a small mud ridge stopped its flow. As we walked further down the path, the sound of the running water began to fade into the distance and the path had begun to widen and flatten out. I scanned every gap between the trees, looking for any signs of her. That's when the handler suddenly slapped his hand on my wrist. I looked at him, his eyes were wide in panic.

"What?"

"There" he lifted his large hand and pointed to the edge of the ridge. I squinted my eyes, and I felt all my breath leave me. There was my mother, lying on the mud floor. The top half of her body was submerged in the water, the other half was spread out across the muddy terrain. I ran to her, and in terror, lifted her face out of the water and set it on the ground. She was soaking wet; her clothes were dirty, and her body was ice cold. I flung my jacket off, tears began to stream down my face, and I struggled to get my voice out. "Mum! Mum!". She looked like she was asleep, as if all the pain and anguish had finally left her. I wrapped her up, I took her hand, pressing it deep in my palms, rubbing it to warm her up.

"Do something!" I wailed to the handler, who was standing at a side, glaring down at his feet. I held her in my arms, pulled her close to my chest, and continued to rub her hands, talk to her, anything I could think of just to see her eyes flicker even for a second. But they didn't. I placed my head in my hands, trying to stop the thoughts and feelings cascade me, but it felt impossible. I was fighting a continent of emotions, the barricades on my land weren't enough to stop the invasion. I cried into my sleeve. Sami ran over and joined me at my side. Like a mother that rocks her child to sleep, I too had returned the favour.

"I'm sorry Mr Roman" the handler whispered under his breath. "This was the way she was found".

"So why didn't you send for help?!" I screamed. "Why would you get me and not a doctor?!".

"Mr Roman, I checked for signs of life. There were none. What could a doctor do?".

I swung my gaze back at her, continuing to talk into her ear as if I was telling her stories and asking her to wake up as if she could hear. She had not moved, nor blinked and in those early hours of the morning as the sky lit up like a candle and birds had come out of their nests and swarmed in the canopies above me, my mother had breathed her last.

Her hands were rigid, the warmth in them that so often caressed my cheeks were gone. The smile that had become a stranger to me looked like it had now reflected in the sky, and with her death, everything that I once was, died too. And yet she was still so beautiful. I continued to squeeze her tight, whispering and praying and cursing and yelling. I told her about my dreams, everything that she would miss out on. I told her about my feelings, asking her to come back because I couldn't replace her as a mother to Meira. I asked her to forgive me because I was ignorant, I couldn't see that she was hopeless, that she was an ember that had been put out and that she was walking in an empty shell, giving every piece of what she could to her children, leaving behind nothing for herself.

"Mama…. please wake up…I beg you. I'm so sorry. I'm so sorry!" I wailed, my cries carried through the trees so loudly that even the animals and insects in the forest stopped in their tracks. "You need to be there. You need to watch me get married. You need to see my first child. You'll miss everything! You promised you would never leave me!".

Sami put his head on my shoulder, whispering that he was sorry in my ear. At that point the handler had ran back the way he came. Whilst I sat, holding my mother in my arms it was as if a revelation came to me. I noticed something that I hadn't seen before. As my vision slowly became less blurry and my heart had slowed down, I noticed a pool of blood around her abdomen. Quickly I lifted her dress to find a gaping wound in the left side of her stomach. The blood had dried out, but the puncture underneath looked fresh.

"Sami? Look".

I showed Sami the wound and he looked at me in horror. We didn't say a word, but we knew…my mother was killed…

A long time had passed by the time the handler had returned. With him he brought a doctor of Naghaar, some Naghaari's and a few handlers. I could hear the commotion, the whispering of Naghaari's trying to guess what happened to her, giving their opinions, their solutions to how her death could've been prevented. The doctor walked over, bent down, and began to examine her. I didn't say anything about the wound. I wanted to see whether the doctor was trustworthy. I waited for his answer.

It didn't take him long to stand back up and announce that she was dead, and the cause of death was…murder…"
I couldn't fathom it. Although, I was aware she was aging, I never once thought that my mother would one day no longer be here. It was the sort of thought that was obscured to me, I had always pushed it to the back of my mind, deep in a subconscious vault that I never accessed.

Until it happened. This vision suffocated me. What were her last moments like? They must've been so lonely. She must've suffered so much.

I felt as if there were simply no tears left, my eyes dried up, the back of my head thumped, and my heart slowed down so much that it felt like I cried myself to my grave. That was what that moment felt like.

"Those Pariah's are ruthless".

I blinked back my tears and shot an intense look at the handler that said it. "They're murderers"

"We don't know it was them" Sami spoke up.

"Who else would it be?" the handler argued. "They've been killing Naghaari's by the number recently. I'm sorry to say Mr Roman, your mother was another casualty in this war…"

They began to whisper among each other and then the

handlers looked over at each and nodded discreetly. "We'll inform Makni Armis about her murder. Those Pariah's will pay. We'll set up the funeral arrangements…"

"Let's cover her, shall we? We need to bury her…" Sami spoke in the quietest tone.

"I don't believe them…"

"What?" Sami questioned.

"I don't think it was the Pariah's Sami. I rejected Makni Armis' offer to take my pledge sooner. He wasn't happy about it".

"Kalei…I don't think…"

"No…" I cried. "Something isn't right. You don't know them Sami like I do. They would do anything to solidify their own name. They killed my mother as revenge. They have a reputation to protect, don't you know? And anyone who disrespects them…they pay the price…"

It was as if I had an epiphany. Makni Armis found a foul, cruel and disgusting way to show he had an upper hand against me. He thought by taking away something I loved, I would follow him devotedly to his grave. But he was wrong. In this type of world, only one thing happens. The subjects would always remain subservient to the rulers. Unless something changed. Unless the subjects decide to take matters in their hands and transform the dimensions of society. That's what I was going to do. I was going to let them know that I would no longer let them rule.

The end of the line

Talia

Tamin had disappeared into the bathroom, and I made my way down to the kitchen to make him food. I began to strike the match, cupping my hand around it to keep the flame bright. It fizzled out. I struck it again and brought it close to the logs, letting the flicker gently disperse into the wood and create a larger flame that I could cook on. As I walked over to pick up the metal saucepan, I felt a warm uncomfortable trickle down my legs. I gasped and pulled my trousers down to see blood streaming down my thighs. I began to panic. Quickly, I rushed up the stairs just when Tamin was making his way down.

"What?!" he yelled.

"Nothing. I need to go to the bathroom".

I quickly brushed past him, ran into the bathroom, and locked it shut. I began to pace back and forth, constantly looking down at the stain that had now formed between my legs. I began to bite my nails, fidget with my hands and it felt as if no matter how deeply I breathed there was just not enough air in my lungs. A loud thump came from behind the door.

"Open the door!" Tamin yelled. "Now!".

What could I do? I had told Tamin that I thought I was expecting but now…my monthly menses had arrived. This meant…oh no, I wasn't pregnant. What would he say? Would he forgive me for my innocent mistake? Would he give me another chance to conceive a child? What if he decided to send me to the zone because he had enough of me?

"Open the door now!" he screamed through the wood. Just

as I was prepared to open the door, an excruciating sharp pain bound around my organs and made me double over in agony. I winced, slapping my hand over my mouth to try and muffle any sounds of pain.

"Talia! I won't repeat myself!".

With all my might, I lifted myself up, my body had suddenly felt like anchors pulling me into the deepest oceans. With my hands shaking, I unlatched the door and Tamin pushed it open.

"I called you so many times!" he screamed. "What's wrong with you?".

"N…nothing. I just…wanted to be sick that's all".

He inspected me in a way that made me feel as if I was on a pedestal, naked and exposed.

"What's that?" he pointed to my trousers. I shot my head down; the stain had gotten larger and darker. "You're bleeding Talia!" he shouted. "Let's get you to a hospital"

"No!" I replied, terrified that the doctors would confirm

what I already knew. "I'm okay".

"That is not okay! Are you hiding something from me?" he hissed, bringing his face close to mine. "If this is a sick way of you hurting our boy God help me, I will get them to brand you right here and now!".

He snatched my hand and pulled me so hard I felt like my shoulder would detach at the bones. I sobbed and screamed at him to let me go, but he continued to drag me as if I was a bandwagon, down five streets as the neighbours watched from their windows. Blood flooded further down onto my ankles and onto my feet. The anguish that travelled through me felt as if my bones were glass, my spine were jagged blades and it had felt like the lining of my stomach had been wrenched through a grinder and lacerated into pieces. My top had slipped off my shoulder, revealing some skin, I felt dirty, obsolete. But Tamin had no care.

By the time we reached the door of the hospital, my trousers had turned from grey to an almost black shade. My wrist was a deep red and burned from the grip that Tamin had on it. My tears had engraved a passage down my cheeks, and they were so dry I could feel the shape of them every time I moved a muscle in my face. All my fears came flooding in through the dam I tried to build in my mind. But it was of no use. I had been submerged.

For the next few moments, I was in and out of consciousness, as if the lifeline of my heart went flat then began to fluctuate and bring back air into my lungs. I opened my eyes to the white ceiling. I tried to sit up agonisingly, but I could only sit up so far without being pulled back down again. I looked down to my left and my hand was bound to the metal bed frame with a thick brown rope that left scratches in my wrist. I began to panic. I scanned the room. It was all white. With what was left of my strength, I tried to tug and pull my hand out of the restraint, but it was of no use. It was so tightly wrapped than any attempt to slip my hand out would take my skin with it. To my right there was a small mirror, about the size of my fist. In that moment I saw a fraction of my reflection. There was blood around my lips that had dried and was peeling and crusting off in flakes. My skin looked parched, aching for some hydration. My eyes looked so tired and gloomy, and my nose had traces of old blood too. I looked at myself blankly trying so hard to remember where I was or what had happened. I glanced down at my legs, realising that my body was shaking with the cold and the goosebumps were so prominent like dimples on a coral reef. My trousers were pulled up to my knees so that the bottom part of my legs was bare, and the blood that had been flowing down them had now stained and dried, leaving long red streaks like slits down my skin. And then I remembered what happened…

I had been taken to this room in the far corner of the hospital wing. Naghaar hospital wasn't large, it had only three floors and the doctors here were rumoured to be from beyond the forest and desert. They spoke with a strange accent, much more refined and complicated than ours. They had an air of confidence in them as they walked, and a strict demeanour hidden behind their surgical masks. They had bound me to the bed, *they*, because I couldn't recall who exactly. Tamin had walked in after me as I screamed and thrashed and pleaded them to let me go.
"Give me a minute with her" he muttered in a grave tone.

The male who I assumed was the doctor, a tall, square shouldered man, who had rectangular frames that sat on his head and two women stepped out of the room and closed the door behind them.

"They told me that you were never pregnant".

"W…what?" I fumbled for my words. "What do you mean?"

"Don't act innocent you dog!" he screamed so loud that I jumped, my pulse thudding with such intensity I was sure my heart would rupture any second.

"You lied to me" he gritted through his teeth. The veins in his temple were plump and palpitating with fury. "The doctor just told me, that blood, is a sign that once again, you have not conceived. You are a liar. You never wanted to be pregnant. You never wanted a boy!".

I could see his hands fold into fists, and he dug his nails into his skin that it left visible marks. Unexpectedly, he approached me, and I retreated into a ball, cowering, and shaking in fear.

"You are disgusting" he spat. He lifted his hand and struck me across the face. I fell back onto the bed and cried out in distress. I tried to shuffle back, but the rope kept me firmly in place. He approached me again, and I tried to protect myself by using my free arm as a shield. But it was no match against his large frame, he struck me again and my ears rang with an intense piercing that disoriented my senses. The pain that spread across my face, burned, and my skin seared as if it had been pressed with a hot iron.

"I didn't do anything!" I screamed. "Please! I promise I'll give you a child next month!".

"This doll of mine is useless!" he shrieked.

All I remembered after that was a large body sat on top of me, squeezing all signs of life, he punched, elbowed, and spat on me until finally I was salvaged by a black raven's wings that masked my vision in darkness. And here I was. Looking at myself in the small reflection, trying to escape the blinding white of this prison like room. I was extremely skilled at dissociating myself, but the last few hours were too much for me to bear. I thought what the world would be like if I was not in it. I thought whether anyone would miss me if I was gone. My parents didn't come to see me since I moved, I had no friends, Kalei even felt like a distant memory and the earth felt like a vast isolated space, and I was just a worthless specimen walking on its ground.

I began to hate myself. My body. For the past few hours, I picked apart every flaw I saw in myself. Just like I used to do.

My eyes were too large, my thighs were too thick, and my stomach was bulging that no clothes could fit attractively on me anymore. I felt useless. I thought whether I was a woman at all if I couldn't even have a child? My stretch-marks were silver contaminations on a once pretty canvas, and my face had lost the essence of bliss, replaced with a silhouette of a ghost of a girl who was once alive. I wasn't afraid to admit that I pondered over thoughts of self-annihilation, but the only thing stopping me from making that a reality was that I had no wish to evoke the fury of God. But the fact that I was still breathing meant that my time on this earth was not yet over. But even after I told myself this, I still couldn't find a reason for me to stay. I had nothing left here, so why was I still haunting the soil of this land?

My face was throbbing in pain. I thought about everything. I could tolerate Tamin's swearing and cursing. I could tolerate his laziness and the way he scolded me constantly. I took a few large gasps of air because, there was a tortuous ache that was extending into my spine. I had an overwhelming urge to go to the toilet but with no way to get there, I sat on my heels and let my body bleed into the sheets of the hospital bed.

And then I heard the lock click, and in walked the doctor and the nurses. There was no moment to pause or think, they rushed to my side and the two women pinned my right side down, and the tall male doctor pushed my left side down. My breathing became desperately fast paced and I was panicking because I knew what was coming next. As they held me down, a man wearing a black mask walked into the room, followed by Tamin behind him. Tamin stared at me in a way he had never done before. The man with the mask, had a long blue robe and in his hand was a steel rod with a glowing tip on the end of it. I could hear the sizzle of the metal from where I lay.

"As a handler, the duty has been bestowed upon me to brand you, Talia Arman as a Pariah. You are hereby removed from Naghaar on the condition that you are not able to provide a male child for Tamin Shodar. Once you have been branded, any association with a Naghaari is now severed. You are no longer deemed a valuable member of our society".

"Dad?" I whispered under my breath. "Is that you?".

The man looked at me intensely, I was so sure that his voice sounded too familiar. I hadn't seen him since I had gotten married, and his presence made me somehow believe that there was a way out of this. He would free me.

The man walked over and stood next to my head. At this point, tears flowed into my ears, and I tried so hard to break out of their grips.

"Dad please" I whimpered. "Don't do this to me. Please! I promise I'll try harder!".

I swung my head at Tamin who had barely blinked since he had been in the room.

"Tamin!" I screamed. "Please! I promise I'll give you a child. Give me one more month! I will try harder!".

The handler leaned in and then murmured in my ear. "It's too late Talia. I always knew you'd be a disappointment". And with those words piercing my heart, dad lifted the rod and pushed the searing end into my forehead. My scream was piercing, the pain was unbearable. And though it only lasted a few seconds, my body shook from the intensity of the heat, my skin had been scorched and burnt and I passed out from the shock of it all.

The zone

Talia

It took me a long time to adjust here, but here I was.

I was a Pariah.

The morning, I was brought here, it felt as if I had died and was resurrected in a squalid replica of hell. Or what hell probably looked like in my mind. I desperately tried to convince myself that I was in a dream, I was still holding onto hope.

The Pariah zone, although so close to where I used to be, felt a million miles away. Not just in distance but in appearance and smell. The floor around here was littered with scraps of paper, apple cores and what was perhaps mud or something else that was brown and soft. I grimaced at the thought of what it could be. The grass was short, brown, dry and prickly as if even the nature on this side of town couldn't blossom at all. I saw rows and rows of man-made dens built only a few centimetres apart.

Each den had a transparent sheet of plastic covering it, but some dens were completely roofless. Others had a bunch of branches lined up, side by side as a makeshift roof, though they didn't look very stable at all, and rain would surely trickle in through the gaps.

Every den was different, the one to my far left had an upside plastic bucket to what I guessed was used as a sitting area of some sort. Another den had no buckets, but only a wired bin with burnt chars of newspaper in it and scraps of fabric used as what I assumed were doors. It was as if I stepped into a different time zone, a different planet. It was overwhelming that such a place was so close to the lavish homes of Naghaar that I could still see across the wired fence. In Naghaar, women had the luxury of wearing a variety of designs, prints and fabrics everyday if they were lucky enough to have been born or married into the rich. Here, women wore mainly the same colour, black, grey and white. It was as if there was an unseen line dividing the colour and colourless.

The zone was deathly quiet, apart from the sound of a few women yelling, and there were a few birds circling the treetops with the distant sound of the Ondas River gushing underneath the logs and slopes nearby. Ahead of me I could see the opening to the Naghaar forest, though I couldn't see anything beyond the greenery, I could feel the loneliness, pity and desperation around me. The horrid smell of faeces, mud and wet cement distorted my senses, and I slapped my hand over my nose so I wouldn't retch. The one place I had always been afraid of, the one place I had never wanted to be was exactly where I was.

That first day, I remember waking up and weeping loudly because I realised where I was. I wiped my tears with my dusty sleeve and threw myself onto the ground and lay flat on my back. I stared up at the grand blue sky, its beautiful canopy was the only thing that I now shared with Naghaar.

"Why are you crying?" came a delicate voice. I sat up and turned to look behind me. A beautiful tall woman was staring down at me. Her eyes were an enchanting shade of sea green, and her brunette hair was loose and reached the nape of her neck. She had pink pale lips, and her skin was a stunning patchwork of different shades of whites and browns. The woman's whole left arm was severely burned and so the skin had turned a dark brown almost black colour and had crusted and flaked in places. She knelt until she was eye to eye with me and then she smiled. Her eyes crinkled, and only then I could tell she was older than me. "Can you speak?" she asked, placing her hand lightly on my shoulder. The woman looked around, looked up at my head and then stared deeply into my eyes. "Are you new here?"

I nodded; I was not proud to admit to it.

"I have some honey in my den"

I looked at her perplexed. She then pointed to my head.

"For the skin. It helps it to heal quicker".

She then lifted her hand and gently felt my forehead, I winced in response to her touch. I then copied her, lifted my hand and touched my forehead. I could feel that the skin was harder and bumpier, a horrible contrast to the smooth skin I was used to feeling on the rest of my body. Although it only hurt when I touched it, I could feel the skin tighten every time I lifted my eyebrows, just like how sandpaper felt.

"My name's Zafinah. If you need me, my den is there" she pointed to the den with the fire set alight in the bin and two huge rubber tyres around it. She smiled, rubbed my shoulder again and walked away.

I was taken aback by her demeanour. Weren't Pariah's supposed to be violent murderers? My parents would always tell me about the story of the Pariah girls, school, the neighbourhood, the whole town would call these girls witches, demons and a threat to the stable structure of society. But Zafinah didn't seem like she was any of these things? Yet I was now a Pariah. I was a Pariah. It took a few times of repeating the words to myself for them to sink in, though I was far from accepting my reality. I realised now that I couldn't rely on what I was taught, I had to learn to live, I had to learn to bloom unaided. I stood up carefully, my legs still felt weak under me. I limped across the soil, scanning the area around me.

Everything was out in the open, women bathed in the open, they hung their laundry using the wires cut out from the fence. There were large buckets for urine and one for faeces, but although the space had felt like an invasion of privacy, everything and everyone seemed to live in harmony. I watched the women, many of them glanced over at me, some ignored me, and others stared at me so severely I had to look away in discomfort. Many women wore tattered aprons that were wrapped around their hips. Some had long dishevelled hair with clumps of mud and twigs in it. Some women were completely pristine, with shiny black boots, pretty, clean dresses that made it difficult to guess they were a Pariah. One could easily mistake them as a Naghaari that had snuck into the zone and attempted to blend in.

As I walked around the dens, on the other side was a large fire, and I was shocked with what I saw. Many of the women, around twenty of them were gathered around it. Some warmed their hands up, others dried their clothes, and the rest ate food together. They had white plastic plates in their hands, and they gathered around a large metal pan that hung on top of the open flame. It was bubbling and boiling but I couldn't say that the smell coming from it was pleasant. I saw them take the single wooden ladle and scoop out a grey looking soup. One woman poured it in for them, and they bowed their heads in gratefulness. They were ordinary women finding peace in their misfortunes.

"Looks pleasant, doesn't it?" came a voice from behind.

Zafinah reappeared.

"Y…yes…I'm surprised" I answered.

"Ah yes different from all the stories you've been told?".

I didn't say anything in response.

"After we get branded, we're taken straight here by the handlers, right? Well, many women never make it. We find them in the woods a few days, weeks or in some cases years later"

"I don't understand…" I whispered, shocked by what I was hearing.

"Naghaari's have a lot of secrets. One of them is that the handlers have killed many Pariah's on the way to the zone. They actually started the war. That's why there are not as many women here as you think there'd be".

"But what about the Naghaari's killed in the forest recently?"

"You mean the council member that died recently?"

I nodded.

She sighed. "He came to the zone to see a Pariah. It's the same Pariah he's been seeing for the last few months. Anyway, he sent away the handler that was escorting him. So naturally, a council member was in our zone, unarmed, unprotected. What did you think was going to happen?"

It made sense. I didn't say anything.

From the corner of my eye, I noticed an ancient woman. She wore a large black shawl around her shoulders, her hair was a dull grey shade and she had extremely thin cheekbones that had sunk into her face. Her eyes were dark and sat deep into her eye sockets and the skin around her eyes and lips were like sheets of paper, peeling and hanging off her face. Around her neck were an assortment of stones of different sizes, strung together with a thick piece of thread with matching stones on her saggy earlobes.

"That's Elda" Zafinah continued noticing how I stared over at her. "Since we were cast out, we needed to create our own rules. Elda was the daughter of one of the first Pariah's. So, we treat her like royalty. Anything you need, she's your woman. She's sort of like our archaic great grandmother resurrected from the grave".

Zafinah scanned my face, I could see her eyes immediately freeze on my fresh wounds.

"What happened to your lip and eyes?".

I turned my head away in shame, the cuts on my lips must've still been fresh and visible from the beating that Tamin inflicted on me.

"You should really use some honey. Come".

I followed her back the way she came, I was afraid of trusting a random woman, but I had nowhere to go, no one I knew, I needed a friendly face to help me adjust because it was all too much. She walked into her den, and I followed close behind. Her den was much more spacious on the inside than on the out. She had a few wooden plates in the corner, and a large yellow blanket that was neatly folded on top of a mouldy mattress. In the other corner were three dresses, that was probably all she had. As I stepped inside, I brushed past some metallic pots, they were severely dented and muddy but looked just about useful enough. Through their reflection, I saw my face for the first time. My eyes immediately noticed my new scar. I caressed it with my fingers, tracing the outline of the ~~PA~~ as softly as I could. It was a deep purple colour, the skin was scabby, wrinkly and nothing could hide it. It was hideous. Every single woman here had the same mark on their forehead, but all of them were of different colours and visibility depending on how long ago they were branded.

It was as if the branded skin was a permanent reminder for a woman that she was not enough for society. That she was worthless and every time she looked in a mirror or came across her reflection in the stillness of the forest rivers, she would remember all her pain and all her struggles and wonder why her disability, her empty womb, her strong will or her ailing health were inhibitors to her living a good life.

Then I realised something, that the handlers could've branded women on their arms or their legs or even on their chests, but a mark on the forehead couldn't be hidden, and that was the whole point of it.

The scar would be visible to all as if a woman's sins were displayed for all the 'good' people of society to see. As if she was cast out of a heaven that she could've been a part of but failed to do so all because she was different. And now that scar was all that separated me from the town of Naghaar, the only thing that prevented me from a peaceful life.

In the chaos of my thoughts, I hadn't noticed the single tear that fell from my eyelash, and when it touched the skin of my toes it pulled me back to my meaningless existence. "It takes some getting used to" said Zafinah as she pulled up her mattress to reveal a small mud hole where she had hidden a small carboard box.

"First tip, create a place to hide your things, everyone here steals them, but I trust you" she smiled as she knelt and began to dig through it. As she rifled through the items, she pulled out a small selection of items. She didn't have many possessions, a small purse that looked handstitched, a piece of fabric with the initials Z & A on it and a small, tattered teddy that had one eye missing and holes in its torso and feet. Beneath all of that were a few bandages, dried herbs and two tiny tubs of mustard and honey.

"I love mustard" she chuckled. With her small finger, she scraped a tiny amount of honey, closed the lid and then proceeded to gently wipe it on my forehead. I grit my teeth, trying to tolerate the pain of my fresh scar.

"Why are you being nice to me?" I finally asked.

She finished wiping my head, then looked me straight in the eyes with a sincere, genuine look.

"I remember my first day here" she sighed as she sat back and started her story. "Within the first few minutes, some women ripped the clothes off my body. I walked around naked for days, starving, cold, close to death before I decided to turn into an animal like them and I stole someone's dress off the laundry line. It was the first thing I had ever stolen in my life".

I listened and watched her as she stared down at her hands.

"That's how you survive here. By fighting to live"

"I'm sorry" I whispered.

"Many of the stories about us are complete fabrications. We're not murderers. Yes, we fight for a reason, we do kill but only to protect ourselves. Naghaari's have been killing many of us, many of the women are scared to go into town to work because of the way we are treated. We are not monsters Talia; we're banished souls searching for our heaven".

I could see Zafinah's chest rise and fall and her eyes blink back tears quickly before they managed to fall down her cheeks. There was a silence between us before Zafinah spoke again.

"Stick with me. I didn't even ask your name!" she sniggered

"Talia"

"Hmm, lovely name"

"How long have you been here?" I asked

"Eight years" Zafinah answered, "so to be honest, it's all I know. My life in Naghaar is a distant memory"

"What happened?"

Zafinah glared at me as if the question was a little too personal, she then retorted, "well why are you here?"

I bit my tongue and didn't reply.

"Too personal huh? Well, I won't say until you do…" she

glared down at my trousers, and I quickly crossed my legs in mortification. I had completely forgotten about the stain.

"I've got some clean clothes…" she smiled.

"Oh and Talia, welcome to the Pariah zone".

After that, I began to follow Zafinah around religiously. Every den had two or more Pariah's living in it; Elda was the only one to have a den to herself. Women threw themselves in awe of her, upon her death, it was said that Elda would announce a successor to rule the zone. Elda had the first option to everything, first bite of food, first drink of water, first choice of new clothing, she was their sovereign in a way, but Elda was clearly impeded by her age.

She had been in the zone since she was seventeen. Elda got casted out because she had developed a mysterious illness, one that affected her skin. Her skin began to peel, bleed and flake off her skin. Bits of her flesh were found in every nook of her home. Her husband found it disgusting and appealed to Laris Roman and she was branded and sent here. Zafinah mentioned that Elda often talked about her experiences, but most recently she had begun to lose her memory and tended to repeat the same things repeatedly.

Another Pariah, Jodie was a baby when she was sent to the zone. A five-week-old child was willingly given up by her parents because her head was misshapen, and her eyes were wider and deeper than a 'normal' baby. It was no surprise, Zafinah pointed out, that Jodie and Elda always sat together, and she only ever saw Elda smile when she was with her. It seemed as if Elda took it upon herself to become Jodie's guardian and Jodie glued herself to Elda's side. I wouldn't be surprised if Jodie succeeded Elda.

After listening to Zafinah talk about the history of the Pariah zone, it triggered an intense feeling of misery within me. I felt utterly disgusted that I was a part of the stigma against the Pariah's. How could Naghaar allow the inhumane treatment of these women? And me being a woman, how did I allow myself to become so brainwashed? It's true when they say you only understand the injustices when it happens to you, just because everyone else conforms, does not mean it's right, and just because nobody speaks up does not mean it's not worth speaking about.

One evening, around a week later, I was sat under the canopy of stars. Zafinah had gone to bathe near the river, the idea of standing stark naked in the dark did not appeal to me, so when Zafinah asked me whether I wanted to wash I respectfully declined. It was true, I felt completely filthy, like an alley dog that ate scraps from restaurant bins. I was not used to smelling like this, looking like this, I was definitely not accustomed to a mouldy mattress and flies, insects and spiders making their home in the place I was supposed to sleep. I was used to luxury, hot baths, maids to clean up after me, I couldn't even recall the last time I ever had to get my hands dirty in housework. From opulence to simplicity, God really wanted to teach me humility.

But I couldn't sleep peacefully. In fact, I don't think I slept for days. Everything I had ever known had changed. The world around me was now all wrapped up in nature and although I had always been one with nature, this type of greenery was not serene. Gone was the colour of the bright white buildings, or the polished golden mantelpieces in my living room.

I thought of my mother who I had not seen for so many months. Did she even think of me? I wish there was a way for me to know. My father who never gave me the affection I needed. I could never forgive him for branding me, even though every fraction of the daughter in me wanted to patch things up. But how can I fix something that was always broken? And Tamin…how could he throw me into the chokehold of malice? Because of him I lost my strength, my conviction, and any belief in my self-worth. And what about Kalei? Maybe my absence would convince him to somehow rescue me. What if I went to the meadow? It was a risk., I could be seen, but what if I did?

I cried into my sleeve. The darkness is an eccentric place, it amplifies your reflections that it becomes self-damaging and dangerous, every sentiment is more potent in the dark. Yet the darkness also has the power to protect, and right now the darkness, the one place I used to be afraid of finally resolved to help me, it concealed my vulnerabilities under its shadowy blanket.

I sat still, the thoughts had dissipated. I gazed through the fence at the other side. It was pitch black. I could hear chirping and skittering but not much else. I looked behind me, there were no women around. I stood up and began to pace back and forth. Perhaps if I paced, I would find it easier to sleep. I watched one foot follow the other, I traced patterns with my fingers in the soil, I stood, sat, jogged, crouched. Nothing eased the restlessness. The air was much chillier, and I had begun to lose a little sensation on the tips of my fingers. I looked beyond the barrier, it was strange, I couldn't explain it, but I had an overwhelming urge to go into the forest. I don't know what came over me, I don't know why, but I made my way to the gates, slowly lifted the iron latch, and ran into the forest. I looked back several times, keeping my eye on the silver of the fence, I wouldn't get lost if I kept my eye on that. It was a reckless action, exploring the forest when Naghaari's could easily see and kill me. But I had to find the little girl in me again, she was the only one that could keep me lucid. So, I ran, and ran and ran.

As I ran into the arms of the one place where I could spread my wings without feeling like they had been clipped, I disconnected from the zone, the feeling of not belonging anywhere and I forgot to keep my attention on the silver of the fence. It had disappeared. I was deep in the forest.

I hoped you were there

Kalei

For some reason, I hoped she was there. Under the willow tree. But no. It was the third funeral in my family in such a short time and it was the first time I waited for Talia under the willow tree. I needed someone; I needed her. My heart was broken into a million pieces, and only she could fix it. But I knew I was being ridiculous. She was married now. She had everything that I falsely promised her. So why on earth would she come back to me?
I would sometimes stand at the corner of her street, watching and waiting to see if she came out of her home, but she never did. I saw her husband, Tamin, alone in the markets,

but she was never with him. I was in unmendable grief, after losing my mother I felt so displaced, so lost. A few weeks after my mother's burial, I sat down with Sami to talk through everything.

"So my pledge is this week. I turn eighteen in a few days…"

"How do you feel?" he asked.

"Numb. I don't give a damn about the council" I gritted. "I just want the bloody money and I want to leave Naghaar. I can't spend a single second more in this town. They are corrupt and heartless".

Sami stared at me and twiddled with his thumbs.

"I understand" he murmured.

"I want you to come with me"

Sami shot his head up.

"Me? To leave Naghaar with you?"

I nodded, I no longer wanted to be here. I wanted to go.

"I…I don't know Kalei…"

"Sami!" I pleaded with him. "Look at how your father treats you! You don't deserve this! We can go live our dreams. Like we always said!".

Sami scrunched his face in confusion.

"How would we do it though?"

"I don't know!" I yelled. "I don't care. We'll just run. We'll just keep on running! Before they find out, we'll be long gone!".

"Are you sure about this Kalei?" Sami asked seriously.

"Yes" I replied without hesitation. "I've never been surer of anything in my life. Since that day my mother said I could, it's been the only thing on my mind. I already knew I was going to take the money. I was just waiting for the right time".

After a brief pause, he smiled and then replied, "okay then Kalei. I'm ready".

I couldn't help but feel guilty, however. My mother was supposed to escape too. I couldn't help but feel I would be leaving my mother behind. Would I ever be able to visit her grave again? That same evening, the letter from the asylum arrived, saying they were accepting my mother's admittance. I shredded the letter into pieces, and if that wasn't enough, I burnt them too. The mark of the ashes remained on the floorboard. But then, my breathing became intense, and I became more aware of the way I was breathing. As if breathing became difficult. And then I began as if there wasn't enough air in my lungs and that I would die right there and then. I couldn't turn off my thoughts, they made me panic even more and God knows how, but after a few moments of taking long deep breaths I was finally able to calm down, though my hands continued to shake for the next hour.

Ever since the day I told Meira about leaving with the pledge money, we were closer than ever because she knew she wouldn't have to live this way for much longer. Sami too, every time I saw him, he had fresh new bruises, but he smiled, genuinely smiled because he knew he would never have to suffer at the hands of his father again. It felt as if everyone's happiness lay on my shoulders. There was a great power in status but there was also a great burden. What if, after everything, I couldn't save them all? There would only be a few more days before I took the pledge, I could do it. I could escape.

Talia

The days passed by slowly in the zone. I slowly grew more confident in leaving the zone after nightfall just for a few moments of serendipity. But I always made sure I stayed close to the silver of the fence in the fear a Naghaari would see me. I had found a perfect route that was concealed and was easy to follow, and to no one one's knowledge I snuck out more often. I would rise early morning because most of the time I could barely sleep. Zafinah would be in a death-like sleep the moment I opened my eyes. Zafinah didn't tell me much about her routine and her 'jobs' as she called it, but every single night she would come back staggering with tiredness until her legs could no longer shift her body any further and she would collapse onto the mattress and drift into deep sleep almost immediately.

During the day, I would follow her and watch what she did. She would dress herself in the morning, using the reflection of the dirty pans as a mirror. She would always scoop out a small glob of honey and massage it onto her forehead, and she started doing the same to me. Then, she would take the honey and drench her scabbed arm in it, rubbing it into every crevice of her damaged skin. I had once again asked her what happened to her, thinking that we had spent weeks together so perhaps she may have opened up, but the moment I did ask, her expression turned grave, and I decided to never ask again. Every morning, the moment she woke up she would bring us both some food, mostly consisting of wet rice that was still swimming in water and either a slice of stale bread or some wild boiled vegetables the rovers collected from the forest. If we were lucky, the rovers would find mushrooms and wild berries and the excitement of women's faces when they ate that reminded me just how lucky I used to be.

Rovers were like handlers. They would hunt for the Pariah's, they would carry axes and arrows on their backs and they would return back to the zone every evening dragging ripped satchels stuffed with leaves and nettles so the women could make some concoction of nettle soup from it. Rovers were always the strongest women, decorating their faces in streaks of mud to camouflages themselves. Jodie was the leader of the rovers.

Gracie always gave me everything I needed, and I would never have to lift a finger to do anything. I took it all for granted. Bathing, cleaning, day to day chores, all these basic necessities I took for granted, and now that I had only a few morsels of food in front of me, I cherished every single bite that I had, even licking the plate clean as to make sure I didn't waste a single crumb. I would recall how frequently my parents' wasted food, throwing heaps of food after parties and dinners into the bin, only for it to be discarded out into the alleyways for stray dogs to eat.

Sometimes, we would eat beside the stone circle. The smell of bland herbed soup or boiled rice would create a sudden swarm of hungry and desperate women all queuing with plates in their hands. I watched as Jodie organised the lines, sometimes sending some women to the back and shifted other women to the front. I never understood why they were organised in a particular way, and I never asked. Here, it seemed everything was already in place, and nobody questioned anything.

In the evening, I would dip my toes into the stream that was behind the zone, its water was ice cold and sent tingles through my body, but it was refreshing, and the sound took me back to the open meadows and flashes of childhood. I wondered how Gracie was doing. If she was in good health and how she must be missing me as I was missing her. I wondered about Lucia, remembering her dislike of Kalei and that the last time we spoke it wasn't a pleasant conversation. Since I had been a Pariah for a few weeks now, I began to also contribute. I would wash clothes in the river and hang them onto laundry lines. I would wash plates and ask around if anyone needed any help. I would see Jodie watching me as she sat with Elda, whispering and pointing. But I didn't let it faze me. I continued to help as much as I could and by the end of the fourth week, I become so used to everything that I no longer cried myself to sleep at night.

The pledge

Kalei

In just a few short minutes, I would be a member of Naghaar council. I would represent everything that I ever hated about the system. People would look to worship me and see a man who represented the glorification of oppression, inhumane treatment of women and worst of all the acceptance of it all. No matter where my heart lay, my reputation would forever be linked to the system. In 20, 30, hundred years from now, my name would be marked down in history as one of the men that supported it. My daughter, my grandchildren, my whole future would see my name and only curse it. But I had to do it. My hope was hanging on by a single gold thread that weaved through my imagination. It patched up my anxieties, my fears, my pain and held it together long enough until the knock came at my door.

"They're ready for you" a handler said.
I took a deep breath, told myself that I was doing the right thing and then exited my house and within moments I entered the council chamber. The next few minutes, handlers rallied around me, each one of them putting on a piece of clothing on my body.
First the blue robe that was silky and slippery, that hung loosely on my shoulders. Then the hat, that was tall, heavy and dug into the skin on my head. And then the long rod, the same rod that handlers used to brand the women of Naghaaar, recently heated in fire, glowing and sizzling

beside me. My hands shook, and I tried to hold my head up high, trying to put on a face of pride.

Makni Armis entered the room, he shuffled towards me, smiling and placing his trembling hand on my shoulder.
"I always knew you'd be a great asset to Naghaar. Welcome my boy".
I stood there, in the full attire, watching and listening as Makni Armis read out the terms and conditions. I lifted one hand and begun to take the pledge.
"I Kalei Roman, hereby, fully acknowledge and accept my role as a member of Naghaar council. I shall follow the customs and traditions as per set out by the great Laris Roman. From now on, it is my responsibility to ensure that every woman in Naghaar adheres to our rules, and it is now my responsibility to fairly deal with Naghaar's matters with impartial and balanced views".

I gulped before I continued reading.

"If any rules as outlined in the pledge paper are broken, I accept full and fair punishment".

And that was it.

All the months I waited for were all over. All the council members hugged me, congratulated me and announced my official appointment to the large group of Naghaari's that were waiting outside. They gave me flowers, bowed their heads, gave me letters and I nodded and smiled and waved as if I was the proudest man in Naghaar.

That evening the celebration for my appointment was held. A marquee was set up where the market stalls usually were. A large cream tent was strung up, with gas lanterns and candles illuminating the inside. A long wooden table was set up, enough to seat all the members and glistening metal plates were set out in every place, meticulously cleaned with forks, knives and spoons that were measured and placed exactly the same distance away. Straw placemats decorated the table, with red cotton napkins and fresh flowers from the meadows. Purple hyacinths, bright yellow sunflowers and bright blue Lobelia's that only grew in large bunches in wet soil near the Ondas River were scattered across the light brown oak. The accompanying stools, absent of backrests, were oak too, and were covered with squares of brown matted fleece that although added comfort was not practical. One seat was left empty, in memory of Ure.

It was extravagant. Makni Armis had also paid a string player from the city to join the feast, and he sat with three others in the corner with their feet perched up on tiny oblong footrests with their violins and guitars resting on their shoulders and knees. They played a delicate tune, stopping occasionally to sip water from a glass or to stretch their necks and backs. I proceeded to sit down but Makni Armis insisted that I must sit beside him. I walked over to the end of the table and sat down as Makni Armis proudly looked right down the middle of the whole table.

Five courses were given. The starter was poached egg with steamed vegetables, with the middle of the egg turning to liquid as soon as my knife sliced it open. The second course was a selection of shellfish steamed in a soup, emulsified with a variety of herbs and spices. The third course was a rump of lamb, braised in a thick juice of some sort, tied with threads that were intertwined with sticks of rosemary and finished off with sprinkles of black pepper and salt. The fourth course was a palate cleanser, a simple white soup that was lemony in flavour and washed away every taste that I had on my tongue. And the final course was a rice pudding, generously cooked with fresh lard and chunks of cinnamon. Once we were done, the servants, cleared the table and brought a large ceramic kettle of fresh tea. The kettle was beautiful, painted with green intricate shapes of leaves and ivy vines with tiny matching ceramic cups.

"My daughter is turning thirteen this year" mumbled one of the members as he sipped his tea.

"Ah…so she's developing I see…" another man chuckled.

"I expect a perfect man for her. If no one bids…I'll bid for her…" he sniggered.

The men laughed.

"How are her bosoms?" another member asked.

"A good size"

"As long as she's not fat" another member joined in.

"She'll never be sought out if she's too fat".

"No no" the first man replied. "A good size".

"My daughter is too plump" a man sitting beside Makni Armis said shaking his head. "I've told her mother to do something about it, but what can she do? She's fat too!" he laughed, sending the rest of them in a fit of laughter.

"As long as she has perfect skin and thick hair then it's okay"

"What about you Kalei? What do you like in a girl?"

"Huh?" I shot my head up.

He repeated his question.

"I…I don't know…"

"Do you want my daughter?" the man asked. "She's thirteen yet but I promise she will grow into a good body, and she'll give you good children" he smirked.

"Send her to one of us and we'll judge her" Makni Armis interrupted with a congested laugh. "Get her to stand in the council chamber, we'll judge her potential…"

"You didn't give your answer Kalei…"

I bit my lip, confused and disorientated at what I was hearing. These men were talking about their own daughters, talking about vile acts regarding their own daughters. I could feel a pit in my stomach, an uncomfortable one that made me want to retch all over the fine linen.

"A good heart I guess…" I muttered.

"Perhaps Kalei here could take your fat daughter, I'm sure she'll lose some weight with him" Makni Armis scoffed.

"No thank you" I answered with a straight face, not entertained by their disgusting remarks.

"You're so serious Kalei. Lighten up. If women are not for producing children, then what are they for?"

I clenched my fists under the table, I could feel the blood rushing to my face.

The council members began to pass cigars around the table. They offered me one, but I shook my head.

"What about the Pariah's?" one of the members asked, lighting his cigar with a dimly lit match.

"It's serious" Makni Armis added. "We must prepare, make sure we have enough weapons and of course the handlers must continue to patrol Naghaar as efficiently as possible".

"May I be excused?" I interrupted.

They stared at me; I could feel Makni Armis' glare sear my skin. I no longer wanted to sit in their company. I felt numb, I felt as if I didn't belong there at all.

"No" he said coldly. "This is your celebration Kalei Roman. Your grandfather was a part of this and now you are a part of us too…"

So I held my breath, dug my foot into the ground just to try and curb any desire to run away and sat very still.

Very still.

The stone circle

Talia

I filled the rusty wooden bucket with fresh river water and made my way out to an area behind the dens where I would mostly be covered behind the trees. Although it was dark now, the embers from the fires that Pariah's lit up still illuminated parts of my bare skin. I asked Zafinah for one of her spare pieces of fabric so I could cover up my body every time someone passed by. The water was ice cold every time I poured it over myself, so I had learnt that I needed to pour it in small amounts just to stop my teeth chattering and somehow lessen the rate at which my legs were quivering. I never bathed at night, I would normally be asleep in my den by now, but I had been washing clothes all day that I needed to bathe desperately.

I was extremely uncomfortable, the women on the other side of the river were openly bathing, as if all their sagginess, marks, cuts, bruises were nothing to be ashamed of. But I was ashamed of my body. I hated it. All my mother's cruel words and all of Tamin's critiques had latched strongly onto me, I felt as if I was in a separate world to it. It was hard to explain the feeling let alone comprehend it. Often, I wished to go in with a pen knife and remove the cells in my brain that wired such unhappiness into me.

"Be quick!"

I jumped as several women ran across, pointing and shouting at a commotion that had broken out. I dropped my bucket, the rest of the water sunk into the ground and some of it trickled down to merge with the river. I quickly scrambled for the fabric in embarrassment, tugging, yanking at it panickily so that no one saw my body. I quickly threw on a freshly washed dress and stumbled out of the leaves and followed the group.

I dashed around the corner and to my surprise the stone circle was lively and active. I had never seen it like that before. Two women were fighting in the circle, bare handed, throwing punches and grunting and shouting. The rest of the women were spectators, gathered around the circle cheering and whooping, including Jodie, who was standing with her arms folded but no expression on her face.

"What's going on?" I asked a short woman beside me.

"This is how disputes are settled"

"I don't understand…" I murmured shaking my head. The woman rolled her eyes as if she was frustrated that I didn't understand her the first time.

"Elda created these rules many years ago, because women used to fight often. Elda took it upon herself to change things here. She decided that the Pariah zone should be equal because the world these women lived in before was not. So, every evening, women fight if they want first claim to food, and they fight for literally anything they want claim to first. You've not seen this yet?" she asked surprised.

"N…no…does that mean I have to fight?" I asked worried about how my lean body would fare in a duel.

"Only if you want to. But if you're happy to get leftovers then you don't have to" she shrugged. "We don't get food gifted to us. We fight for it…".

She stared at my confused face, and then she asked.

"You're Zafinah's girl, aren't you?"

I nodded.

"I see…she didn't tell you…" she scrunched her face and turned away.

"What?" I asked. "Tell me what?"

"Where do you think your food was coming from?" she sighed.

"I…Zafinah said everyone gets it…."

"Then you're dumber than you look" she expressed sternly.

"Wait…are you telling me that Zafinah has been fighting in the stone circle every evening so I could have food?"

I gasped at the sudden realisation I had and the complete obliviousness I had for so many weeks.

"She fights every evening…" she responded. "I guess you know now…"

"No" I shook my head. "If I knew that I would've refused".

I turned my body and sprinted back to my den, angry and confused at what Zafinah had been doing for me. I stormed into the den, where Zafinah was applying honey to her scabbed arm.

"Talia?".

"Why didn't you tell me?!" I yelled.

"Talia…slow down…what's happened?".

She stood up and walked over to me.

"You've been fighting in the stone circle so I could eat? Every single night? That's why you've been coming back late? And that's why you're always tired?"

"Talia…" she clasped her rough hands around my shoulder and squeezed my skin.

"I didn't want you to know. You're my responsibility".

"I don't want to be" I refused. "You don't owe me anything, in fact, I should be the one repaying you for everything you've done for me!".

I pulled my body away from her and swung my head away.

"I will not be a burden" I whispered. "Don't worry, you'll never have to do that for me again…"

"Talia please…" she cried. "I don't do it because you owe

me anything…I do it because…because…" she sighed deeply and took one step back, resting her arms by her side.

She walked back to where she was sitting, and then dropped down, not looking up at me.
"You somehow remind me of my daughter…" she muttered. "I don't know how…but when I saw you that first time, something in me saw what my daughter would've grown up to look like…"
She stared up at me, tears welling in her eyes. "Your eyes, so beautiful and brown, that's what hers were like. Your pale skin, so soft, like hers. Your thick dark hair reminded me of her too. Everything about you reminded me of her. And something in me wanted to protect you in a way I couldn't protect her!" she began to cry into her hands. I stood still. I didn't know how to react. After a

moment, I walked slowly towards her and knelt beside her. I pulled her hands away from her face, I wiped her tears with my fingers and cupped her face in my palms.

"Oh Zafinah! I'm so sorry!".

I threw my arms around her shoulders, and I could feel her dissolve under my embrace.

"My mother never loved me as a daughter. If I had a mother like you, I know I wouldn't be in such despair as I am right now" I said.

Zafinah blinked back her tears and then pushed me away. "I know you've not told me about your marriage…but he didn't realise how blessed he was to have you as his wife".

"Thankyou…please Zafinah" I begged. "Teach me how to fight. Teach me how to hunt. Everything. I want to start fighting in the stone circle. I want to be strong…"

For five whole days, Zafinah took me into the depths of the forest. We first began with a knife, a blunt one. She taught me how to push the blade into the tree, as if it was a human torso, and how to pull back my arm in a way that I wouldn't hurt my wrist or elbow.

"How come you never became a rover?" I asked. "You know how to fight. You're strong". We sat down on a large log for a few minutes to catch our breath.

"This..." she pointed to her arm.

"I know how to fight and hunt yes. But my arm, this arm, it's not that strong. So, it's a weakness..."

I looked at it and then back up at her.

"What happened?"

"I had a daughter...". Zafinah gulped hard, physically trying to supress her tears and trying exceptionally hard to push her emotions back down her throat.

"My daughter died nine years ago. She had some kind of illness and she died one day. She was three years old..." she took another deep breath and braced her trembling voice before continuing.

"That teddy that I keep was hers... I know it's ripping at the seams and dirty and disgusting, but it was hers…"

My eyes widened, and I began to sniffle and clear my throat to try and hold back my tears.

"I was sinking in grief after her death, a coffin the size of a basket was lowered in the ground. And my husband blamed me and that made me blame myself. Until one day I had enough, and I set myself on fire…"

There was a long pause before she continued. Her lips trembled and tears began to stream down her cheeks.

"I hated my body too, because every time I looked at it, I saw her. I wanted to kill myself Talia…" she stared deeply into my eyes, and I could see the grief tattooed in them.

"Zafinah I'm sorry…"

"It will be her birthday soon…she would've been twelve…"

"Zafinah…I…I'm so sorry…"
She cleared her throat, wiped her face and quickly went back to her usual self. I didn't know how she did it.
"Come on. Let's continue…"

By the following week, Zafinah had taught me how to set traps in the forest using nets and stones. She taught me which berries were poisonous, which leaves could be eaten without falling sick and she showed me how to light a fire. By the end of that week, I was able to use a knife skilfully and had slowly started getting the hang of using an axe. I struggled with the weight of it, but I no longer held it with trembling hands, I was slowly building my strength. We knew that the war between the Pariah's and Naghaari's had worsened again, and Jodie often talked to the women about the possibility of the zone getting attacked. More women began to be trained in hand-to-hand combat and in weapon use. The older women who had no way of holding weapons or fighting began to support the others by sharpening the blades, creating small bags to carry those weapons and they began to create soups, enclosing them in plastic jars and storing them for future use. If we were ever attacked or ever had to leave the zone, we were a step closer to being prepared for it.

By the end of that week, I was preparing to fight in the stone circle for the first time. But, before I could put what I learnt to use, I had been told something that I didn't know at the time would change my life.

The answer

Kalei

I was sat on a cobbled footstep, directly opposite the market. Men and women attended to the stalls, picking fruit, smelling flowers, and chattering and laughing. The wind had picked up and dry dust on the ground began to swirl and cloud my vision. From the corner of my eye, a young girl approached me.

"Kalei?"

"Yes?"

"I just wanted to tell you something…"

I waited for her to speak. She looked nervous.

"Talia…do you know?"

I stood up and took a step towards her. I didn't mean to come across as intimating, but she shuffled back as if she was afraid of me.

"What about her?"

"She…erm…well from what I heard. She was branded"

My heart stopped in its own beat. The whistling of the wind had silenced.

"A few weeks ago, apparently. I only heard a few days ago. I've been trying to find you"

"Are you sure? How do you know this?"

"Some women were talking about it. I was wondering why I hadn't heard from her in so long. And then I asked my father to ask her husband. He confirmed. Tamin sent her to the zone because she couldn't give him a child".

I settled on one idea, then rejected it. I thought about one thing then tossed it. I was in a loop of toxic thoughts that were sure to corrupt my brain the longer I stood there.

"She was my best friend…" she murmured sadly.

I turned on my heels, ready to sprint across the desert pan, ready to enter the zone with no care about the consequences. But it was as if the girl could read my thoughts, she quickly stopped me.

"Whatever you're thinking…don't. You can't just run into the zone and demand to see her!"

"So I'm supposed to just accept this?"

"You're a council member now… listen…" she leaned in closer so she could whisper right into my ear.

"Go to the zone. Find her. Escape"

I stepped back and traced the expression on the girl's face. "It's risky" I stated, looking over my shoulder to make sure nobody heard. "I…I haven't got my allowance money yet. I get it tomorrow night. I don't know why I'm telling you this…" I sighed. "I was planning on taking the money and leaving Naghaar anyway. I was just waiting for the money".

"Will you take Talia with you?" she pleaded. "She doesn't deserve it. Please, she loved you".

After a long pause I asked her. "How do I get into the zone? It's not like before, when members would just go to the zone and spend private time with Pariah's. There is a war going on now. If I go in there, the Pariah's will kill me…Look what happened to Ure"

The girl looked down at her feet and scrunched her face in uncertainty.

"I'll do it" she suddenly burst out. "I'll go and see her!"

"How?"

"I'm not a threat. I'm just an ordinary girl"

"You're still a Naghaari" I gestured. "You're still disliked whether you're a man or a woman…"

"I know…" she smiled as an idea came to her. "I'll disguise myself as a Pariah…"

"But…"

"Kalei, just write a letter. Write a letter telling Talia about your plan. Tell her a time and place, and once you've got the money, you take her the hell away from here. I'll do the rest".

Before she turned to run away, I shouted after her.

"Why are you helping me?"

"Just take her away from here" she smiled slightly at me, tying to reassure me that everything would be okay.

A few hours later I had secretly pulled Sami to a side, behind the school gates I told him what had happened.

"It makes sense, doesn't it?" I said

"It's risky Kalei…"

"Sami…" I grabbed his arm, excited at the prospect of seeing Talia after so long. "She's in the zone. The horrible Pariah zone. Her husband that…" I clenched my teeth in order to hold back my anger. "I've never stopped thinking about her Sami. I was too late before. I wanted to marry her, but she was already married. But now, I have the chance. I can be with her. More importantly, I can save her from a horrible future!".

"But she's in the Pariah zone" Sami uttered worryingly.

"That's sorted" I acknowledged, brushing off his concern.

"So, this girl, who you don't know, is going to deliver your letter to her? And then what?"

"I've asked her to meet me in a specific place. Two days from now. By then, Makni Armis will have delivered my money and I'll be free to leave"

"You'll be a defector" Sami shook his head. "You're risking everything"

"I'm not staying in this town. I already told you this. I'm not representing a barbaric system like this. My mum…my mum wanted me to settle down with a girl I loved. I love her Sami. I want her".

I could see he was concerned.

"Sami, I was going to leave anyway. But now, I have her to take with me. And you…if you want to? Do you still want to?"

Sami sighed. I could see the worry etched onto his face. "Look, I won't force you. But I don't want to leave my best friend behind. What do you have here? A dad that…." "I paused and then continued. "I will leave my home at 5am. If you want to come with me then bring everything you need but only things you can carry. I don't know how far the city is from here. We could be walking for miles so wrap up warm. I hope to see you then"

"It's so soon…" Sami breathed.

"It's now or never Sami. I can't live another day here. The second I'm getting my money; I won't look back".

I held out my hand to shake his but instead he wrapped his little finger around mine and whispered "adelfi", and I did too.

Everything was going to change.

The letter

Talia

"This is for you" Zafinah said as she entered our den. She held out a letter and waved it in my face.

"What?" I asked

"A girl, there's a girl who gave it. Said it's for you. I've never seen her before"

"But why did she give me a letter?"

"I'm not a mind reader" Zafinah huffed, forcefully pushing the letter into my hand. "Take it"

Talia,

Before you rip up this letter and burn it, I just want you to listen to me. I'm so sorry for breaking our bond. I'm so sorry for ending things between us. I saw you get married. I came to you that day to tell you that I wanted to marry you. My mother died, and she told me to take the pledge and leave Naghaar with the money. She gave me permission. And so, everything's changed.

If you will allow me to, I want to make amends. I will be receiving the money tonight and with the money I'll be leaving Naghaar tomorrow morning. If you forgive me, if you still feel something for me, then I want to take you away from here.

Let's leave. Let's go far away from Naghaar. I really hope you trust me enough. I will be under our willow tree at 6am tomorrow morning. Meet me there.

By God, I hope I see you. And if I don't, just know, you always were and always will be the best thing that ever happened to me

Yours,

Kalei

I clutched my chest; my heart was beating at a speed I was uncomfortable with. Sweat formed on my forehead. God, I missed him. My heart pounded in my ears. Just the thought of an escape, just the thought of finally getting out of Naghaar made my legs quake and my hands shake violently. I would no longer need to bathe in dirty rivers or eat leaves and berries for sustenance. I no longer had to sleep in the cold and worry about fighting in the stone circle. I took a deep breath. Zafinah watched me closely.

"What is it?" Zafinah asked. "What's wrong?
I didn't reply, it was as if I couldn't hear her.
"Talia, what happened?" she repeated.
I quickly pulled her hands and clutched them in my own. She jumped with the sudden way I yanked her arms.
"I'm only telling you this because I trust you…"
Zafinah watched and waited for me to speak.

"I…I'm leaving Naghaar…"

"I'm confused Talia…"

"There's a boy, from Naghaar and well, it's super complicated but I'm leaving with him in the morning, and we're getting out of here. Far away".

She looked at me blankly, I couldn't tell what she was thinking. My heart was thumping. What if she told someone and stopped me from leaving? I shouldn't have done that…

"It's dangerous" she whispered. "It's too risky. What if the Naghaari's see you? They won't hesitate to kill a Pariah"

"I know. But I have to"

"No Pariah has ever left with a Naghaari before. Damn it Talia, you're going to end up killing yourself"

"It's worth it" I smiled. "I have nothing left here" "Talia…" she sighed. "You don't realise, you'll be changing the course of history. Things will never be the same if you do this"

"Come with me." I burst out.

She pulled her hands away from mine and took one step back.

"I can't" she finally said.

"Why not? He's got money, if that's what you're worried about"

"No Talia!" she yelled. "I can't. You're being so stupid! God! I can't!"

"Why not?!" I begged.

"Because! Because that day that the maids saw me set fire to myself, they managed to douse the flames. Only my arm was damaged. I had to live the rest of my life in grief. For days and weeks, I tried finding things to kill myself with, but the women here became my saviours. They watched me, guided me until one day I was alone with a pen knife…I picked it up, but I threw it into the river. That's when I realised, I never want to kill myself again. I want to survive".

"Zafinah I don't understand …"

"This zone, yes, the whole of Naghaar are afraid of us but this zone, these women, they made me who I am today. Because of them I'm still alive. Every time I look at my arm the memories come flooding back. So, I purposefully don't cover it, just to remind myself that I'm strong and that the world once tried taking me down, but I came out of it alive. And ironically that keeps me going". She took my hands again and squeezed them tightly. "There have been months and years I dreamt about escaping but now I can't. This is my home"

"It doesn't have to be" I shook my head; refusing to accept that I would have to say goodbye to her.

"Please" she whispered, her voice trembling. "I need to stay here. It's my home…you can't ask me to leave my home…"

"I don't know what I'll do without you"

"You'll live. You'll live your life in the way my daughter

couldn't. And you stay safe and use everything I taught you. And Talia, you get the hell out of here, you understand? This boy better be worth it".

Zafinah had become a part of me, she had helped me to cope, she had pulled me out of the dark hole I was in. To think that I would leave her behind broke my heart. But she was insistent.

"I may have lost my child, lost my husband, my home, my self-worth and I may have lost my friends along the way, but I thank God because I have gained a daughter in you".

And she held me tight, and I did too.

It was the last time I would ever see her.

The meeting

Kalei

A knock came at the door, I looked back at Meira who was smiling, twiddling her thumbs, eager to get going. It was 5.00am. I opened the door to Sami, and I threw my arms around him. He didn't hug back.

"I'm so glad you're here! Are you okay?"

Sami stepped inside and quietly closed the door behind him. It was pitch black in the house, and the street was eerily quiet. But I could still make out Sami's face, he looked disconnected, he looked heartbroken.

"My sister won't come with me. I tried telling her everything but all she did was scream at me for being a horrible brother and son"

"I don't get it"

"She says I'm a traitor. That I'm abandoning my father and that I'm an insult to Naghaar. She won't come with me Kal…" he looked despondent. His eyes were on the floor, and he looked conflicted with his emotions

"I don't want to force you Sami…"

I put my hand on his shoulder and then he looked up at me.

"No. I want to do this"

"Sami…my sister Meira…"

Sami looked over at Meira who was standing behind me. She looked worried, perhaps because she always imagined what Sami looked like or perhaps because she always imagined what it'd be like when someone out of the family finally saw her.

"It's amazing to meet you" smiled Sami. "I've heard a lot about you"

Meira smiled back, looking over at me then back to Sami. "I've heard a lot about you too" she chuckled. It was strange. I never thought they would ever meet, but now that they had met, it felt strange.

"You guys ready for this?".

They both nodded in response. I walked toward the door and told Meira to throw a scarf over her mouth, just in case somebody saw her.

Although the whole of Naghaar were in their homes, a few more handlers had been dispatched that night and they were patrolling the desert pan looking out for any Pariah's that may be sneaking into Naghaar after nightfall. We had to be quick and quiet. The plan was to lead them to the meadow, wait by the tree for Talia to arrive if she hadn't arrived already, and then to move through the forest, and through the desert as quickly as we could. I knew, it didn't sound like a good plan at all. To be honest, I hadn't thought about what we would do after we had escaped. We had no particular direction we would go in, just the nearest city which had been rumoured to be at least a few miles away. It sounded ridiculous now, the more I thought about it. But we were all willing to leave Naghaar, to go anywhere. To escape our fears, to escape our cages. There was no guarantee that the city we found ourselves in would be any better, but what could be worse than living here?

My mother was no longer around, bless her soul, and I just couldn't see myself in this town, being a council member, condemning hundreds more women for the rest of my life until I went to my grave. I think, we all knew that there was no certainty going forward for any of us, but the certainty of living here was too harsh of a reality for any of us to accept.

As we closed the door behind us, Meira glued herself by my side, her hands shaking from the overwhelming sensations of the outside world. Sami scuttered quickly, moving his feet in panic, looking left and right and over at me. A few minutes passed, and it felt as if every second lasted an hour. We were more aware of every little noise, every sound, and every flickering light. At one point, a dog had run across the path and Meira screamed, threw her body behind me and we stopped for a brief second to catch our breath from the sudden scare.

On my back I carried a brown rucksack, which I stuffed with a few jumpers, a spare jacket, clean socks and food and water. A small side compartment was stuffed with a bag of cash that Makni Armis had personally given me a few hours ago.

"You are our reputation" he grumbled, and I nodded

convincingly that I would uphold that reputation. But as soon as I shut the door, I stuffed the cash into my already packed bag that was hidden beneath the sofa. I had on a khaki wool jumper; it was one that my mother got me a few years ago. It wasn't in the best condition, a few threads had come undone at the shoulder and there was a stubborn stain at the collar, but it had a very faint smell that reminded me of her. Even though I felt as if I was leaving her behind, it also felt as if she was a part of me.

Meira on the other hand had worn a black cotton dress that grazed her knees, paired with black trousers underneath. She wrapped a thick scarf around her face and wore plain white flat shoes that were scuffed and muddy. I had brought that for her only a few days ago as she never owned a pair of shoes. I could see she was uncomfortable walking in them, constantly bending down and digging her finger at the gap behind her heel. Sami opted for a navy-blue jumper with red patches on the shoulders. He wore that with black trousers and a black woolly hat, that fit tightly around his ears so only his ear lobes stuck out. He wore a large black rucksack, that had holes and loose threads and he tucked his thumbs into the straps as he walked with a rapid pace behind us.

We approached the corner of a house, and I held out my arm to tell them to stop in their place. Around the corner, just before the opening of the field, a handler stood, pacing back and forward with a machete in his hand. I glanced back at them, and they stared at me wide eyed. I could see the fear in them. I nodded at them, trying to discreetly tell them that it would be okay. I turned my head to watch the handler again.

"Stay right here. As soon as I say, you run into the forest, okay?" I whispered.

I took a deep breath and ducked out from behind the corner. I walked over to the handler who instantly turned his body to me, tightened his grip around the handle and shouted.

"Oi, show yourself!".

I lifted my hands, as if to say I didn't mean any harm.

"Don't you know who I am?"

The handler squinted his eyes as I approached closer to him.

"Mr Roman!" he smiled and straightened his back. "Sir, what are you doing out at this time?"

I stood next to him and held out my hand to shake his.

"Your name?"

"Jordan, sir"

"Jordan…"

I glanced back briefly, making sure that Sami and Meira were still out of sight

"I have a favour to ask you…I need help…"

"What do you mean sir?"

I cleared my throat, trying to buy a few seconds whilst I thought of what to say.

"I…er…I think I saw a Pariah down there" I pointed in the opposite direction, "but you see, I have no weapons. I think she may have been armed"

"Oh no…of course sir. I will go find her right now. Rest assured that I will ensure you get home safe…"

"No" I shook my head knowing he misunderstood me. "I don't need you to escort me home. I just need you to find that Pariah"

"But sir, I need to protect you first"

"Jordan…" I placed my hand on his shoulder. "Trust me, get rid of that Pariah and you will be doing me a great service. I will personally commend you to Makni Armis"

He smiled widely, pride glowing in his eyes.

"Yes, of course. I will find her. Please sir, get yourself

home. I will remove the plague that rots this town…"
He ran off, disappearing around the corner with the machete raised high in his hand. I quickly spun around, gestured for Sami and Meira to come, and they dashed across as quickly as they could. We jumped behind the trees and out of view.

Talia

My heart was pounding in my ears. I didn't have much to take with me, but just a large old fabric which I filled with one dress, and a few scraps of bread and two cans of soup. I bundled them up, created a small knot and threw the sack over my shoulder. Zafinah was in a deep sleep beside me, and I looked over at her, tears filling my eyes. I leaned over, gently kissed her on the cheek and left the den. I ran, I didn't even bother trying to be quiet, I just wanted to run into the forest as quickly as I could. My feet crunched on crispy leaves that littered the forest floor, the sounds of birds came alive and created a harmonious discord of whistling around me. The sun was slowly rising, with just a faint line of glowing amber appearing in the skyline. I knew 7am was sunrise, I was running late. What if Kalei left without me? What If he waited for me and couldn't wait no more? Surely it was past 6am by now. I was drowning in thoughts, anxious about the possibility of being left behind. I ran, and jumped over muddy holes, and stepped through ice cold streams, soaking the hem of my dress and dirtying my bare feet and legs.

Within a few minutes, I had come to the clearing. I stopped, scanned the distance for any shapes and sounds and then ran across again. Panting, sweating. I could finally see the tree in the distance, and I suddenly felt at ease. I was almost there. I reached the base of the tree and desperately looked around. There was silence, no one was there. I bit my lips, frantically threw my head left and right trying to find Kalei's face. I began to panic, the sun was starting to rise, the amber had now turned to a pale yellow and the white clouds were starting to unveil themselves

"Talia!"

I turned my body, and Kalei jumped out from behind the bushes and threw his arms around my body. I dropped my sack to the ground and wrapped my arms around his neck.

I began to cry, in relief.

"I thought you left!" I cried

"I would never leave you" he muffled into my hair. A few seconds passed, and he gently released his grip around me. His cinnamon-coloured eyes and thick brown hair was a heavenly sight to behold.

"It's' you!" I cried. "It's really you!"

"God Talia. How do you get more beautiful every day?!" he wept.

For a long moment we held each other. There was a comfort that was magnetic, his presence was the clothing on my skin and bones, shrouding my cold body in the warmth of his smile

"Where have you been?!" I cried

"I'm so sorry!" he wiped his tears with his sleeve. "I didn't even know you got sent to the zone! I'm so sorry!"

All the weeks of waiting, the anticipation, the worry, all melted into nothing the moment I set eyes on him. He had done it. He had saved me.

Kalei

She was angel treading the earth, and the time spent not seeing her made me appreciate her even more. I noticed her body, fragile, shaking under my touch. Her hair coarse and dry and her eyes looked tired and exhausted. I would never know how her life had been the past month, but I was determined to make it better right then.

"You didn't give up on me…" she whispered. "Oh God…". She suddenly released her grip around me and turned her body away from me covering her face with her hands

"What is it?"

"How can you love me?" she began to cry again. "Look at me!" she fell on her knees, hiding her face under her palms. I walked over to her, kneeled beside her, and gently pulled her hands away from her face

"Don't look at me" she muttered. "I'm ugly…"

She pointed to the branding on her forehead. She was disgusted with herself and had not come to terms with the way she looked. I leaned in so my eyes could meet with hers. It was the same feeling we always had, and that's how we knew what we had was real. The way our eyes connected were like shooting stars across a crowded moonlit sky. Wild and beautiful. I felt a tsunami of butterflies in the pit of my stomach.

I took my hands and cupped them around her face. I traced her scar with my fingers, across the edges, the ridges and whispered as she watched my lips move.

"Do not let society define what beauty is" I began. "That scar on your head is a mark of a woman that was too strong for a weak man. Always remember, a skin with marks, is a skin adorned, like a painting, every stroke, dab, brush, and splash of colour makes the canvas the way it is. And so do your scars. Don't let anyone damage your extraordinary work of art because of the price tag someone else put on you. You are human, you are a woman, and therefore you are a beautiful anomaly in an ordinary world".

She was a spectacle, encased behind delicate glass, and the scar on her head was not a mark of shame but created a sense of wonder in me like century old cursive ink on a once lost scarlet letter, found sealed with gold wax, but perfumed with the scent of familiarity. For the next few moments, we sat in complete silence, and it was comforting because we were home. We *were* each other's home. That's when I truly realised, I loved her. I loved her. I smiled at her; and then from behind me emerged Sami and Meira.

Talia

Two people emerged from behind Kalei. One of them was a short boy, with round glasses and a thick woolly hat. He smiled slightly at me, and I could see the bridge of his nose pinch when he did. The girl beside him was younger, she had thin black hair that was wrapped tightly in a ponytail. A scarf was wrapped around the lower half of her face, and she looked at me deeply with her soft brown eyes.

"Talia…this is Sami and Meira"

"Your best friend?"

"Yes…he wanted to leave Naghaar too"

Sami half smiled at me.

"Meira…it's a pleasure to meet you. I wish it was under different circumstances" I spoke. I could see she smiled with the way her cheeks lifted. There was a brief silence between us.

"You have no shoes on" she said in a gentle voice. I looked down at my grimy feet and chuckled.

"Come on" Kalei insisted. "We need to go. Even here, we're too exposed. There are handlers patrolling the woods".

As Kalei turned to walk away, Meira quickly ran over to me, pulled off the scarf around her face and handed it to me. She pointed to my forehead, and I understood what she meant. As I wrapped it around my head, I glanced at her lips. I didn't mean to stare, but she noticed, and she quickly lowered her head and turned away from me "You're beautiful" I quickly said, and she smiled, covered her face with her hand and we followed Kalei into the forest.

Into the Forest

Talia

We reached the edge of the river where the water was much more aggressive and where bark, leaves and branches were rapidly taken away downstream. To get to the other side, we had to cross a large mud-covered log. Its edges were deeply rooted in the ground, so it looked steady enough to walk over, and unlike many logs that looked covered in scale like chips, this one was smooth and brown. In the past hour, it had begun to rain, and everything was soaked and muddy. Every time I walked, the mud beneath me squelched, we were wet and cold, and our clothes stuck to our bodies. Kalei had brought an extra jacket, and I wore that, and zipped it tight to contain what was left of my body heat. I shivered with the relaxing wave of warmth I suddenly felt.

"I'll go first, and you follow" instructed Kalei, lifting his large boots and gently finding his balance on the thick birch. He glanced back at me, and I gestured to him that I was ready. I looked behind me, Meira was shaking, with her hands cupped tightly around her ears, the sounds and sights around her must've been too much for her to handle. Sami was behind her with his hand grazing her back for support. We all followed Kalei closely behind. Halfway across, the log began to slightly wobble, Kalei looked behind him to find me flailing my arms around to try and keep my balance. I groaned and muttered that I was fine, pushing Kalei's hands away that were outstretched for me. Suddenly, my foot slipped, and I stumbled and fell.

"Grab my hand!" Kalei shouted, urgently trying to grab to stop me from falling into the fast-raging river. Meira and Sami shouted out from behind me, I clambered onto my feet quickly but kept slipping on the log's surface. I grabbed Kalei's hand; it was firm and strong and within a few seconds I was back up on my feet. We all managed to cross over, with Kalei standing in the middle of the log helping everyone along. We jumped off the other side and safely embarked. As the rainfall increased in intensity, the log began to wobble more intensely, and it slowly began to slip off the ridge. I took a deep breath and wiped my wet hands on my muddy dress.

"Let's go under there, until the rain stops. That river will soon be flooded".

Kalei pointed to a large tree, its leaves drooped over and provided a good shelter for now. We all ran over and huddled under it, sitting on the floor in a circle.

The sound of the rain pattered on the leaves and some managed to trickle through the gaps in the canopy and onto my forehead.

"I always imagined what the rain would feel like" Meira spoke from under her breath. "I imagined it would be warm, but it's unpleasantly cold" she shuddered.

"Main thing is we stick together and stay hidden" Kalei spoke. "We need to get out of the forest as soon as possible"

"How far is it?" I asked.

Kalei shrugged his shoulders. "I know it's not too far to the edge, but I have no idea what will be on the other side"

"It's the desert, isn't it?" I asked

"Yes. But I don't know how long it would take to cross the desert"

"It doesn't matter" Meira interjected. "We're safe once we get out of the forest. Naghaari's don't go beyond the forest anyway"

"Sami?" Kalei looked over at Sami who had been sat quietly, with his legs tucked into his chest. He looked up and smiled. "Are you okay?" Kalei asked.

"I don't know..." Sami whispered. "What if I made a mistake? My sister...I condemned her. I didn't even bring her with me"

"You couldn't have forced her" Kalei replied, putting his hand on Sami's shoulder. "It's not your fault"

"What am I thinking?!" Sami stood up and began groaning loudly in frustration. "I left behind my sister. I left behind my father!"

"But your father..."

"My father is a monster yes! But he's still my father!".

I looked at Kalei who looked guilty for bringing Sami along. I could see in his eyes that he was terrified that Sami would go back to Naghaar. Terrified that he would lose him.

"Sami..." he looked over at Meira. "Look at me..." she

gestured to herself. "I never once left those four walls. How do you think I feel? We're all sacrificing something, but we need to escape the familiarity of home to find happiness…"

"She's right" muttered Kalei. "Your father didn't love you. Otherwise, he wouldn't have done what he did to you. We all have regrets Sami, but if you don't escape right now, you will regret it for the rest of your life. But if we dwell on all the things that could've been, we would be lost in our thoughts for an infinite number of lifetimes. And we only have one life Sami"

"Look at me…" I continued. "I grew up as an item, I was sold. I got branded because I couldn't have a child. This isn't my body anymore. But I'm trying to reclaim it back".

For the next hour we all spoke, revealing all our fears and dreams. Although it was the first time, I met Sami and

Meira, I could see exactly why Kalei loved Sami so much and I could see a reflection of Kalei in his little sister. We sat and talked like that until the rain stopped, and as we spoke Kalei told me how Lucia apologised for everything. How she wanted to feel love and that's why she was so against the idea of this. I never even got to say goodbye. At least Kalei could take Sami, I couldn't do anything for Lucia.

Kalei

To my relief, Sami had agreed that he would stay with us. I stared at Talia who avoided looking me in the eyes. I knew she was broken by a man who only wanted pieces of her and although I could try to put them together again, they would never fit like they used to, there would always be cracks in between the place she broke. I wanted to show her that I could be the one to make her whole again, but there was so much of her I still never knew, and so much of me she never knew. But there was something comforting about all of us together in one place. The way we all spoke as if we'd known each other for years. Talia and Meira were laughing and smiling with one another, and Sami seemed to finally relax and had become used to the idea of leaving Naghaar.

As we stood up to leave, suddenly there were distant yells and screams. We panickily looked around, staring into the distant to see what or who it was.

"They've found us" Sami cried.

Before we knew it, we were all running through the forest, in a random direction.

"How did they know?!" I yelled as we dashed through the trees.

"My sister…" Sami screamed back. "It must've been her. I can't believe it!".

Found

"Makni Armis! We have an emergency!".
A handler ran into the tent, never would he have done that on any other occasion, but this time there was no attention given to the rules of courtesy.
"This better be worth it!" shouted Makni who had just sat down and been served a piping cup of tea. The handler quickly called in a young girl, who dashed in, bowed her head and proceeded to talk.
"Our supreme leader…I have the gravest news!" "Speak!"
"My brother, Sami, informed me early this morning that he was planning to run away from Naghaar"
"I don't see why this is an issue" Makni grumbled, putting the cup of tea to his dry lips. "We've had so many boys leave Naghaar. Get rid of her!" he spat
"No no!" she begged. "Not just leaving alone, leaving with

a council member. I didn't think he was telling the truth but when I woke up, he was gone"

Makni slammed the cup down, tea spilled all over the tray, with some staining his white robe. He grumbled and groaned as a few other members quickly helped him up.

"Who?"

"Kalei Roman"

Makni Armis' demeanour changed, and he shuffled as quick as he could to the handler, rage burning in his eyes. "You go to Kalei's home now! If this be true, he is a defector, an insult to the very name we have so sincerely upheld. And if this be a lie…" he glared at the girl and stiffened his jaw. "You will pay for the disrespect of entering our tent in this manner and for trying to taint a council member's name…Go!".

Panic spread through the town. It was around 8am and every Naghaari was now out on the street. The news of Kalei's defection sent tidal waves of shock, and handlers had gone to his home and pounded on his door. After several minutes, and no reply, they smashed and kicked the door down and found his wardrobe empty and no sign of him. There was cussing and shouting and swearing and when the news reached Makni Armis, he threw his hat in rage, he kicked the cabinets as hard as his old legs could muster and he spat and cursed Kalei for what he did. Because not only did the news reach him that Kalei left town, but Makni Armis found out that a Pariah went with him.

There was a loud commotion that burst through the streets of Naghaar, and everyone was in shock at what the grandson of Mr Roman did.

"I want him found!" screamed Makni Armis. "But be sure that pathetic Pariah girl is killed and bring Kalei to me alive. I want to teach that boy some lessons!".

The largest manhunt known to Naghaar had begun. Handlers armed themselves with knives, bows, machetes, and axes. They seeped into the woods, searched every inch of the town. Everyone known to Kalei had been meticulously questioned and then when Makni Armis posed the question, "if anyone knows anything about the Pariah, speak now. You will be rewarded immensely". No one said a single word, until Naghaari's entered the Pariah zone and began beating up Pariah's to extract information.

A handler approached Zafinah, who had just woken up to the sound of screaming and shouting. They pulled her by the hair and dragged her out of the den. Two by two, every single Pariah was lined up outside of their dens, and Honum, Makni Armis' lead handler entered the zone. He was a tall gruff man, with a large scraggly beard and a mauve birthmark on his left cheek. He walked around the zone, inspecting every Pariah, inspecting every den. He walked up to Elda, towered over her small fragile frame, and demanded for her to tell him who was missing. Elda refused, insisting that she had no idea who was missing. Honum slapped her, sending an uproar of screams and cries across the zone. No one had ever laid their hands on her. This was an insult to the Pariah's to see Elda being treated in such a way. Again, she refused, and Honum struck her again, this time much harder and the old woman stumbled back and let out a cry. Jodie ran to her side, begged Honum to stop and blurted out Talia's name. "She's the only one that's missing!" she screamed. "Please leave Elda alone!"

Honum smirked, turned away and made his way back to Makni Armis.

The following announcement was given, anyone who found Talia Arman would get a lifetime supply of money. The largest sum of money known to any man. Tamin had heard, and insisted he wanted to join the manhunt, Talia's father Nico also insisted on joining even after her mother begged and cried for him not to join. Almost every single man in Naghaar, joined the hunt, Talia was the prey and Kalei was simply ordered to be arrested.

As for Sami's sister, she asked Makni Armis to spare her brother, she only wanted him to return home, to which Makni Armis replied, "we don't punish men for the sorcery of women. We will return him home safe".

As for the Pariah's, they began to arm themselves. Elda had a large mark on her cheek, and she was panting heavily from the shock of Honum's slaps. The Pariah's couldn't handle such an insult. And so, they grabbed weapons and began to prepare for the real war.

Night one

Kalei

The next hour was the most terrified any of us had ever felt. The shapes and sounds around us were a blur. Our heartbeats were thumping, pounding, beating more times than it was capable of. We scampered through the woods, throwing glances over at everyone's petrified faces. Sami ran close behind Meira, she was panting and panicking, and swinging her arms. Talia's eyes were wide, she ran quickly behind me, and the scarf over her head had fallen off and landed on the ground behind us. That mark on her head was a target. More than anything else, Meira and Talia had to be hidden.

"Here!" I yelled, pointing off to a small path on the left.

We ducked under low lying branches, stepped over loose logs and jumped over muddy puddles and slippery surfaces. We came to a clearing, to the left was just more forest, thick and green and anything beyond that was barely visible.

"We can't keep running!" gasped Sami.

"Come". I instantly sprinted towards the bushes and crouched behind it, concealing my face under its thick greenery. They all followed and did the same. A few minutes had passed, agonising minutes, the screams, rustling, shouting, footsteps were much closer now. In the dim light I looked over at Talia who had tears running down her cheeks, one hand over her mouth and Meira's hand rubbed her back. I watched her eyes widen; more tears stream down as she tried to stifle her sobs. It was then I realised she was looking at something, or someone. Approaching us were three men. One was large and round, with thin hair brushed back revealing his large, flat forehead. The other two were smaller in comparison but glued themselves by his side.

"Are you sure?"

"Yes" the large man replied in a gruff voice. "The scarf wasn't too far back. They must've gone this way"

Before they ran past us, the man grabbed the other with a tight grip.

"Remember she's mine" he snarled. "I want to kill that doll with my own hands. Something I should've done before". And they all ran down the path and disappeared behind the trees. None of us dared move. Afraid they would reappear any second. Afraid that if we made any sound, they would find us and that would be the end of the dream that had just started.

"Talia…" I whispered as quietly as I could. "Are you okay?"

I could see her hand that had covered her mouth was drenched in her tears, her eyelashes were soaked, and her cheeks were burning red. She removed her hand and gasped for air. She took three long deep breaths, and I held out my hand to rub her shoulder.

"Tamin…" she muttered. "That was him…"

This was not good. This meant a manhunt. This meant that Makni Armis had found out and had given an open invitation for every man to look for us, not just handlers. We were in extreme danger. It was hard enough to escape handlers, but it was possible. But to escape almost a hundred men scouring the forest…I was truly afraid.

"It's okay" I reassured them all. "It'll die down. By nightfall they'll stop searching"

"What do we do until then?" asked Meira under her breath

"We wait…"

Talia

No matter how much Kalei tried to hide it, this was more serious than we could've imagined. Tamin would not be out looking for me unless Makni Armis ordered it. I was a target. And that meant I had to watch every movement in the trees, listen intently to every rustle and snap and keep my eyes open when the sun set. It was approaching nighttime and at this time, Zafinah would've usually lit a fire with dried leaves and twigs using two arid sticks. But I was no longer there, I was no longer with her. Instead, I was here, worried about the risk of being seen by anyone.

We lay on the ground; my back was against Meira's and Sami's back was against Kalei's. We kept our bodies attached, hoping that our body heat would survive us through the night. I used Kalei's jacket as a blanket for Meira and me. She shivered behind me, and I tried to rub her legs with the back of my heel just to try and give her some heat.

It had been a while, but eventually Meira and Sami had fallen asleep. Kalei refused to sleep, stating how we had to take turns to make sure nobody found us. I watched as Kalei stood up and groaned quietly as a sharp cramp shot up his legs. The sky was pitch black and I could barely make out the shape of his face let alone where his eyes were looking. The air was now colder, and everyone began to shiver slightly. I could hear his stomach begin to growl, and we realised it had been hours since we ate. He dug his hands into his pockets and felt something hard. He pulled out the apple he picked up when he left his house that morning. He considered sinking his teeth into it. It still looked bright red and juicy, and his empty stomach was now at the forefront of his mind. Before he did, he looked up at me, paused, bit down on his lip, and then walked over to me.

"Here. You need all the strength you can get".

I sat up slowly, careful not to wake Meira up who had thrown her arms around my hips during the night.

"You need it more" I whispered.

"Halves?" he smiled.

We sat on the ground, and he shuffled his body close to mine. One by one we took a bite from the apple; he ate from his side, and I ate from mine. Quickly, the apple core was exposed, we glanced briefly up at each other and chuckled because we both had started to take the tiniest bites so that the other had more to eat.

"Come on Talia. Take a bigger bite"

"Not until you do".

Although to a strangers' eye, this moment seemed trivial, to us it meant a lot. After everything, we still cared more about each other than ourselves. In the chaos of everything that was happening, we still managed to find some form of happiness in the shape of an apple core.

A couple of hours later, Meira had awoken, closely followed by Sami. I guess, we were all restless, constantly worried someone was watching us. I sat under a tree, with my head on Kalei's shoulder. There was just something about his presence that calmed my nerves, especially after seeing Tamin

"So you never went outside, ever?" Sami asked Meira. They were sat opposite one another. Meira was twiddling a muddy leaf in her hand and Sami just watched her. It was not quite sunrise but there was a delicate light that brightened the lower half of the skyline. Enough light that we could make out each other's expressions.

"Nope. Although I had tried a lot recently" she chuckled, looking over at Kalei who smiled back.

"I never wanted anything more than to escape too. Though both of our reasons were completely different".

Meira crumpled her eyebrows and tilted her head slightly to the side.

"Why did you never tell Kalei?" she asked Sami. I felt Kalei's shoulder stiffen at that question, as if he was suddenly paying attention. Sami shrugged his shoulders.

"I was ashamed I guess…"

Sami turned his head to Kalei.

"I was ashamed because you had everything. You lived in luxury, whilst I could barely afford enough food for school.

I was ashamed because you never hesitated to give me money even when I never asked for it. And I was ashamed because the day your father died; I wished mine did too. What kind of human did that make me?"

"A normal one" Kalei responded.

He sat up, pushed himself off the ground and walked over to where they were sat. He kneeled in between Meira and Sami and placed his hand on Sami's knee

"I wouldn't care what you told me Sami. You are my brother. Whether by blood or not, I would've done anything for you"

"I know…I just always felt…less than you"

"You may have felt less but you were always worth more to me than my life Sami"

Sami smiled, and I could see his body relax under Kalei's touch. I could see their bond, it was natural, completely visible to the blind eye. The amount of times Kalei wished he would be a better brother to Meira were endless, but I don't think he ever realised that although he felt like he never did enough for her, and never was enough for her, he was enough for Sami.

Suddenly Sami burst into tears.
"I'm so sorry Kalei. About my sister!"
Kalei quickly pulled Sami into a hug and squeezed him tight.
"Don't say that. We don't know it was your sister who told Makni about us"
"She was the only one who knew besides us!" he cried.
"You're not responsible for her actions Sami, okay?".
A few moments had passed, and Sami had wiped his tears, and the boys were laughing once again.
Meira lifted herself up and slowly walked over to me. I smiled, non-verbally telling her that it was okay for her to

sit next to me. She sat herself down and sighed loudly.

"He really loves you; you know?" she finally said. I giggled.

"He really loves you too"

She lowered her head and rested her chin on her knees.

"How can he love me after everything I put him through?"

"What do you mean?"

"Trying to sneak out. All the horrible words I said. After losing mum…I watched him suffer, and I happily added to that suffering just so he could feel the same way I did"

I lifted my hand and gently stroked back a strand of her hair.

"We all make mistakes Meira. But the main thing is, you're trying to make amends. Trust me, he always talked about you. Always talked about how much he wanted to protect you"

"I'm not surprised that he didn't tell me about you. Why would he? I was not close to him…" she sighed. "How did you guys meet?"

"At your dad's funeral"

"You must've taken his breath away. I've never seen Kalei like this around anyone before. Well, how could I? I never left the house" she laughed. "Can you marry him?"

I sat speechless. I had no other reaction but to laugh at what she said, I had no idea if she meant it or not.

"I'm not joking" she firmly insisted. "He needs to marry you…"

I shook my head.

"I don't think that's on any of our minds right now…" I chuckled.

"I wish my mum was here. If she knew you, she would've made you her daughter right there and then…"

"That's sweet of you to say. I'm sorry about your parents. It must've been so hard" I said.

"I blame myself…" she sighed.

"Why?" I questioned.

"Because my mum was…" she shook her head. "I just

made everything harder for her". Meira's eyes instantly changed, she frowned deeply and began to dig her nails into her palms.

"I'm a monster. I'm a monster!" she yelled. She shot up, glaring down at me. Kalei and Sami quickly turned their heads too.

"Meira…what happened?" Kalei asked concerned.

"I…" Meira pointed her finger at herself. "Mum died because of me!".

Meira began to cry and pull at her hair. She marched back and forth, and Kalei ran to her and desperately clutched onto her arm to calm her down.

"Shh…" Kalei begged, frantically looking around. "We need to be quiet. Meira…calm down. It wasn't your fault!"

"Shhhh…" Sami shrieked. "I can hear something!".

Kalei

There was a loud rustling and something in the trees moved in an eerie way. Although there were moments of brief silence, the air felt intense. All of a sudden, two handlers jumped out from behind the trees. One of them, with an axe in his hand, began to swing for Talia, she jumped back and shrieked, and I slammed my body into him, and we fell to the ground. I began to wrestle him, using all my strength to push him down and keep him down. He tried to use his free arm to overpower me, but I was able to grab the axe from his hand and throw it away. I sat on top of his chest and began to throw punches at his face. I could hear screaming behind me, but I didn't look. I continued to land large blows on his face, before he stopped fighting back and went limp and passed out. I gasped and caught my breath.

I stumbled back up and groggily turned behind me. Sami was being pushed up against a tree trunk by the other handler, and Sami, much smaller in height and weight was bleeding from his nose. Talia held Meira and they cowered behind the tree, panicked, and terrified. I ran over, grabbed the man by the shoulders and pulled him away from Sami whose blood had now stained his shirt. Again, I pushed him, tackled him to the ground and hit him continuously until he too groaned, winced and fell unconscious. For a moment, I stayed where I was, trying to catch my breath, trying for a moment to calm my shaky nerves and attempt to ease the way my bloody knuckles trembled.

"Are you all okay?" I panted.

Sami shook his head, wiping his nose and smearing the blood all over his sleeve. Meira and Talia had gently released the grip they had around one another and slowly emerged from behind the tree. Before we could catch our breath, Sami yelled, "there are more coming!".

I stumbled to my feet, we picked up our bags and once again, ran through the trees. We ran more than we stood. We panicked more than we breathed. For the next few hours, we went to several corners of the forest, just to hide for a moment before we had to run again. The Naghaari's had surrounded almost every inch of the forest. Getting out of here seemed impossible now.

Night two

Talia

It was nightfall. We somehow made it another night. Alive. Sami propped himself up against a tree, Meira walked over to him and began to assist him in cleaning up the wounds on his face. She used her sleeve and dabbed on Sami's nostrils, he flinched, asked her not to ruin her clothes but she continued anyway. Kalei was sat on the other side; his eyes scanned the trees. His hands were bruised and bloody and he looked on edge.

"Kalei?" calling for his name made him jump. I could see he was worried and more than anything, I could see he had many regrets.

"It's okay…" I whispered. "We'll be okay".

He turned to face me, and I saw tears in his eyes. They glistened in the darkness.

"No" he murmured. "I don't know how far till the end of the forest. I don't…I don't know what to do".

I placed my hand on his shoulder, but they were tense.

"We can do it Kalei. We'll make it out of here"

"As long as you do" he answered in a serious tone.

He took a deep breath and then turned his full body towards me. He took my hand and clasped it in his.

"I would ask you to be my wife but I'm afraid I won't live long enough to see that day"

"Kalei…what are you talking about?" I stuttered.

"I just…I pictured our life together. Our future"

"Kalei…" I placed my hand on his cheek. "We still have a future. Why are you speaking as if we don't?"

He didn't answer.

The rest of the night passed in complete silence. Both Sami and Kalei took turns in staying awake. I lay on the ground next to Meira, but we couldn't sleep. And even though we closed our eyes, we both knew that there was a chaos of thoughts and worries that were racing through our minds. No amount of sleep could help us escape the fear we had about what would happen the next day, and the day after, and the day after.

Kalei

That night was dreadful. The silence was horrifying yet it was a silence that reminded me we were alone. It distorted my senses that every sound or sight was filtered and examined scrupulously by my rationality. From time to time, I heard scutters right beside my ear that made me jerk back in disgust. I felt a slow sensation of something crawling up my leg, across my chest and slip behind my neck. I jolted, quickly brushing my skin with my fingers, and telling myself that it was nothing. I heard skimming, chirping, slithering, squeaking, snapping and every noise in between. But in this cacophony of noises, I was numb deep down. I felt as if I had trapped everyone.

The truth was, I had no plan. I had no idea what direction we would go in the moment sunlight appeared, I wasn't sure whether we were circling around the same area several times a day and mindlessly causing blistered skin for no good reason. The moment sunlight appeared, I blinked my eyes, I had not slept a single minute. Sami drifted in and out of sleep throughout the night, and I could see him forcing his eyes to stay open every now and then. Talia and Meira slept beside one another, and throughout the course of the night, they had wrapped their arms around each other.

That day we stopped often to rest. We shared some stale bread, breaking a few pieces and distributing it around. It rained most of the day, so most of the day we stayed under shelter. We were soaking wet and cold. There was not much conversation that day. At one point during midday, we saw a group of Pariah's hunting. Talia wanted to ask them for help, after all she was one of them. But I pulled her back and kept her close to me. I was a Naghaari. This wouldn't end well.

We sat hunched on the forest floor, shielded by the green leaves that concealed us. It was now portentously dark, and my body had begun to shiver and tremble with the cold. I tried to move my legs often during that time so that they wouldn't freeze in one place. I rubbed my palms together, every so often bringing them up to my mouth so I could warm them up. The heat dispersed quickly, and I shuddered again. The forest was haunting at night. We had been told stories of the Pariah girls, of the Pariah zone, the killings that happened in the forest and a large part of me was terrified of living away from the rumours and living within the reality that loomed before me. My stomach was rumbling in intensity, it had been around ten hours since we last ate. More than hunger, I was thirsty, my lips were parched. I could've followed the sound of the stream and dipped my hands in and drank, but I was afraid that the lack of light would claim me, and I would break an ankle, or fall into the ice-cold water and freeze myself to death.

Night three

Kalei

I don't know how it all happened or what happened for that matter. But in the dead of night, when the moon was most high, it's iridescent light peering through the foliage, we were running once more. But this was different from the last few nights. There was an intensity that followed us, we were more afraid than we had ever been. Sami was close behind me, and Talia and Meira were running parallel to us just a few 100 yards to the right. Every now and then, we glanced over at each other then quickly darted our eyes back ahead of us. There were 4 handlers behind us, running, screaming, yelling, knowing that the more sound they made, the more reinforcements would come in our direction.

Unlike every other night, this night we were truly unable to escape. Because everywhere I looked, I saw wild faces, hungry for Talia's blood. My fate was unknown and that didn't scare me. It was that I knew Talia's fate, and that shook me to the core. I could hear Sami's panicked breathing close behind my shoulder, I could see Meira's beautiful brown eyes encased in horror and Talia's black hair whipping wildly as she ran. There was nowhere to run. Nowhere.

Every direction was covered by a handler, and after a few minutes of pure fear we were stopped in our tracks. In a dark, dense area of the forest, we ran to each other, and huddled in a group, with our backs against each other. All four handlers had caught up to us and had surrounded us. They smiled menacingly, they watched us and chuckled, holding up their weapons in the air.

"There's nowhere left to run now Kalei," laughed a handler. "Time to hand over the Pariah…"

After a moment, another handler joined in on the fun.

"Look at her!" he cackled pointing at Meira. "How ugly! She can't be a Pariah; she has no mark…so…"

"She was hiding in Naghaar the whole time…" interrupted another handler. "They have made a fool of us!"

"Let's get them!"

"Wait…" one of the handlers put out his hand to stop the group from approaching us. "Let's have some fun first…"

"Please…" I begged. "You can take me, let them go!"

They all erupted into a wave of laughter.

"We don't care about you Kalei. Makni Armis has other plans for you. We're here for her…" they pointed directly

at Talia whose body was shaking against ours.
"You'll have to kill me to get to her" I demanded. "Same" Sami answered.

I glanced over at Sami and smiled. My brother was with me. The handler nodded to the others and the four of them approached us. They knew we would try and put up a fight. They pulled Talia and Meira away from us, wrapping their arms around their necks and keeping them firmly in one place. The other handler yanked Sami back, his small frame made it easy for the handler to push the silver of his knife against his throat.

I could feel every part of my soul and body dissipate into a darkness I had never been in. I stared at Talia, and she watched me as they dragged her away.

The last handler was a large man. Almost twice my size. He had a clean-shaven head; large black beard and he had a deep scar that ran from the base of his neck to the bottom of his earlobe. He grabbed me and wrestled me to the ground. I tried with all my might and power, but I couldn't break free. He held me down and pinned my face to the ground. Out of his pocket he pulled a rope and began to wrap it around my wrist. He knotted it tightly, so tight that I felt the fibres cut into my skin.

"Meira…just know I did my best for you. I love you my baby sister…" I breathed.

Although I was face down on the ground, I could turn my head to the side just about to see Meira glare back at me. She burst into tears as she screamed back at me.

"I'm so sorry for everything. I love you!"

"And Talia…" I groaned as my restrained hands began to send hooting pains up my arms. "I have and always will love you. Remember your worth".

"No!" Sami screamed. "I won't let this happen!".

Suddenly, Sami threw his body into the handler that had his arms around him, he grabbed the knife from his hand and began to slice and cut anything and everyone in front of him. He shrieked and raged and although he only managed to slice the air, his sudden eruption caused one of the handlers who had his arms around Meira, to run over and assist.

That handler tightened his grip around the machete he was carrying and in the blink of an eye he plunged it into Sami's stomach. There was an overwhelming silence, and my heart had completely been ripped apart. I watched as Sami fell to his knees, blood poured out of every nook and cranny of his abdomen, and it poured down his hips, down to his thighs and ankles. He jolted a few times, glanced down at the gaping wound and pressed it with both of his palms to try and stop the waterfall of red. He looked up at me, tears formed in his eyes, and he managed to force one last smile. "Adelfi" he groaned, barely audible, and he collapsed to the floor, bled out and died right in front of me.

There was nothing I could say or think that could describe that moment. It felt as if someone had yanked arteries from out of my neck and grinded them. My heart rate had completely slowed down, as if I was dying, and my soul dropped to the pit of my stomach. My best friend, my brother, the centre of my universe for so many years had been killed. And it was all because of me. Because I thought we could escape, because I thought money was enough to build a life.

It felt as if life was breathed back into me, and suddenly I began to gasp and take deep breaths, as if my body was in a state of shock. I couldn't control my breathing; I couldn't control the way my body shook. Sweat began to drench my forehead, the back of my neck began to feel intensely hot, and my hands began to tremble rapidly. I heard them yell that during the commotion the girls had managed to escape. But I couldn't see or think of anything else. Except that body that lay on the ground, of a boy that used to be my adelfi...my brother.

Talia

It was an opportunity, and we took it. I never wanted to leave Kalei. I never wanted to run away from the one man I wanted to run to. But, after seeing the way they butchered Sami, Meira had shrieked and cried and told me that we couldn't risk it. The handlers beside us were distracted and at that moment, Meira grabbed my hand and wrenched it. Before I knew it, we were running away from the bloodbath that happened behind us. We were running through the trees. I had so many thoughts racing through my mind. Sami had just been killed. How must Kalei have been feeling? Would I ever see him again? What if they killed him?

No, I had to stop with these thoughts before I got too carried away and sunk into a pit of sadness.

I followed Meira closely behind, and we ducked and dived and weaved through the trees. There were distant shouts of handlers finally noticing that we had escaped. But unless our stamina was made of liquid gold, we couldn't evade them for long. We gasped and panted and stuck close to each other. Meira pointed to a large tree trunk that had overtaken the forest floor. Weeds had sprouted everywhere, and flies were floating in large groups that they had begun to stick to our faces. I gagged and spat out the flies that glued to my lips and flew into my nostrils. We rushed over to the trunk, and I watched as Meira crawled into a little space she found in it. I copied her and clambered onto my hands and knees and crawled in a small space in the side of the tree trunk. It was just about large enough, but I had to squeeze my shoulders as I pushed my way in. The gap was covered with a few weeds and we both sat, legs tucked into our chests and we caught our breaths.

What felt like hours passed, but in reality, it was only a few minutes. We gazed at each other in the darkness as sounds of handlers approached closer. As I sat, a centipede appeared from under the ground. Its long black body slithered up my leg and I shook my leg to get it to climb off. But it continued to walk up my leg, over my stomach and close to my chin. I squeezed my eyes shut after Meira had placed her fingers to her lips to tell me to stay quiet. The handlers were only a few inches away from where we were hiding, any sudden noise would give us away. It crawled onto my head and sat on the base of my forehead. I could feel its legs, like small taps and trickles on my skin. Suddenly, a handler appeared in the hole and began to grab my legs. I screamed and kicked him and shuffled back. Meira began to throw anything she could find, rocks, pebbles, branches. He lost his grip around my skin and reached out for Meira instead. He was too large to fit in here, and so he could only reach as far as his wide shoulders allowed him. He clasped his large hands tightly around Meira and pulled her out of the hollow. I frantically tried to pull her back, but she disappeared out of view, screaming and crying. I didn't know what to do. If I went out there, I would be killed instantly. But if I stayed here then Meira would be battling them alone. I could hear her screams, and the men laughing and cackling. I heard clothes tearing and the sounds of Meira's screams suddenly muffled. I froze. I began to rock back and forth in horror, panicking, thinking of what to do. After a few moments, I braced myself, I was ready for them to turn their attention to me. Before I could, there were sounds of several women screaming. There were sounds of running, jumping, grunting, punching and the slicing sounds of the silver of weapons. There was a commotion and after a few moments everything fell silent.

"You can come out now" a woman's voice shouted out.

"We're not going to hurt you".

I brushed the centipede off my hair and shivered with disgust.

"Talia?" the woman said.

I snapped my head towards the voice, shocked that she knew my name.

"Don't be afraid".

After a few moments, I decided to crawl out of the space. As soon as my head popped out of the hole, I turned to look at a group of women staring down at me. They were Pariah's. I stumbled onto my feet and brushed the dirt off my knees. I scanned around and noticed all the handlers dead on the ground. I ran over to Meira who lay on the ground, cowering. The lower half of her dress had been cut, as if they had attempted to reach her hidden place. "Meira" I whispered, grabbing her head and pulling her close to my chest. "I'm sorry. I'm sorry. Are you okay?" She didn't say anything. She just stared off into the distance. I finally turned to the women.

"Thankyou so much"

"You've really tilted the scales of Naghaar" one of them said. "Your escape with a council member has created something much worse than a war"

"What do you mean?"

"The Pariah zone no longer exists. As soon as Makni ordered handlers to go out and find you, they attacked the zone and tried to kill many of us. We managed to escape…some of us bravely fought…but we were no match for them."

"I don't understand…" I shook my head.

"We're a threat now…the zone is a threat now" another woman interrupted. "Makni sees us as a threat to the stability of Naghaar. He doesn't want to risk something like this ever happening again, so he ordered for all of the Pariah's to be killed. All of them"

"Oh my god" I muttered to myself. "I ruined everything …. Zafinah? Is she okay?"

The women looked over at each other and then back to me.

"No. She was killed"

"Oh no…" tears began to fall down my cheeks. "It's all my fault…"

"You need to go before the rest of them find you"

"No" I shook my head. "There's nowhere for us to go. We don't know where we're going or what we're doing…"

The women looked over at each other and then nodded.

"You can stay with us for now then. But you best be on your way once the forest is clear"

"Can't we stay with you?" I asked

"They can stay" a voice came from behind the trees. Jodie

appeared, carrying a large sack over her back and a holding a long machete in her hand. "They can stay" she repeated.

Day 82

Kalei

I wish I was still sat under our willow tree. I wish I was taken back to the day when I knew I was falling in love with you. I don't know if you'll ever read these letters but if by chance you do just know that I love you. With every crevice of my soul and every beat of my heart, I love you. Don't ever blame yourself for my fate. I'm glad I could be a part of your freedom.

Take that freedom and do something with it. And Talia, never let that scar put your self-worth down. To me you were always beautiful, you are always beautiful, inside and out.

And if I never return to you just know that on the day that I ascend to heaven, whenever that may be, I will thank God for the glimpse he gave me of paradise in the depths of your celestial eyes.

Letter 1

Yours, Kalei

It's been 3 months since the escape, day 82 to be exact. I had begun to scratch lines into the pebbled wall, but the stone I had in my hand was blunt now. The harder I tried to draw with it, the fainter the grey lines were. There was only one gap high above my head where I could see the sunlight. The iron gate that I leaned my head on was rusty and brown and it creaked every time they unlocked it. Which was very rare. The only time they visited was to torture me some more into giving away the location of the Pariah I escaped with. I never broke my silence.

The room was just about large enough for me to outstretch my legs. The walls were a sandy brown colour, and the dust from the town settled in heaps in the corners. The hall was long, and every cell was like mine. There was no bed, the stone floor was my mattress. Once a day, a guard would give me food in a plate, and it was just about 2 morsels of bread and a cup of water. I don't know why they kept me alive. I don't know what they needed me for. Here and there, the chains that kept me bound to the floor, dug into my ankles, and the sound of the rattling began to bother me that I rarely moved my legs in the hope I could sit in silence. The iron reminded me I was a prisoner. Every so often I heard talks of Makni Armis losing his mind. He stayed awake most nights, trying to figure out where the Pariah had gone. It bothered him, it ate him up inside that he was unsuccessful in finding her. He hated to be trumped. But that's what I loved. I loved that the man who created hell for every woman in Naghaar finally felt some sort of anguish himself.

Although I had not seen myself, I could feel that my skin was not the same. I could feel my ribcage when I touched my stomach, and I could feel the coarse dry ends of my hair every time I stroked my hand through it. Hunger had become a friend and thirst had become a close companion. But the pebble I squeezed tight in my palm did wonders for me…it allowed me to draw faint images of the woman who had my heart. I wondered where she was. How she was. I wondered whether she was safe and happy and whether Meira had finally found the freedom she so desperately wanted. The truth was, I didn't want them to miss me. I wanted them to live.

"Cell 14". The iron gate shrieked as a guard pulled it open. I fell back and he kicked me in the back.

"Move" he grunted.

He bent over and pulled me up by the arm. Another guard came and he leaned over and unlocked the padlock on the chain around my leg. On either side of me, they linked their arms under mine and walked me out of the cell.

"You're going to torture me more?" I chuckled sarcastically. They didn't reply.

"There's nothing you can do that will get me to tell you anything. Haven't you learnt that by now?"

The doors of the prison opened and instead of taking me to the left and down to the basement, a route I could easily memorise by now, they grabbed a black cloth and tied it around my eyes. They took my arms and bound it behind my back. I could hear sounds of people talking as they continued to walk me. It was a while of walking; I knew that I was being taken somewhere I hadn't been before. Perhaps they finally had enough of me. Perhaps they decided it was about time they killed me...

After a few moments, the smell of cinnamon hit me. It was completely random, but it churned so many good memories inside of me. It reminded me of my mother... Suddenly, they ripped the blindfold off my eyes, and I winced with the amount of sunlight that almost blinded me. I blinked a couple of times before realising where I was. The council chamber. I looked around and all the familiar faces of the town were staring at me. Talia's parents, Gracie, Sami's sister, Tamin. I could see the grief in Gracie's eyes, she must've hated me for failing Talia. And then I turned to see Makni Armis appear from behind the curtain and trudge over to me. He shuffled slowly and came to a stop right in front of me. Though he looked even older, he had a youthful and fiery anger that burned in his eyes. It had been as if his anger had been simmering and now it had come to a boiling point. He glared at me but didn't say a word.

He turned his body towards the people of Naghaar. "I'm sure you must be wondering why I have called you all to my humble abode…as you all know…this man…tried to escape with a Pariah…"

He scowled at me again and then coughed dryly before continuing.

"So, we never have a repeat of history, we ordered the killing of all Pariah's. I am pleased to say, the forest is empty of those vermin and the zone has been burnt down. And this man, who was supposed to be from the Roman bloodline, has tarnished our reputation with his reckless actions".

My heart sunk the moment he mentioned that the zone had been cleared. He had wiped out a part of the human race just so he could feel whole inside.

"So, I'm proposing something…Kalei Roman after deliberation we have decided…that you are now officially the first Naghaari to die by execution. Though it displeases me most deeply that the first to be executed is from the Roman bloodline, the end of your story will be the ultimate example for people of Naghaar. For centuries to come, this will serve as a warning for anyone who might attempt to do what you did and that if they do decide to go against the wishes of the Naghaar council, it will be met with fatal consequences"

The men yanked at the chains, and I stumbled as they led me out of the tent.

"Makni…"

I turned my body to him. He grimaced at me that I referred to him by his first name only.

"Men like you are not men at all. You can boast, you can flaunt your wealth and you can continue to objectify women. But one day, those women out there, my woman, they will fight back. And when they do, don't beg God for forgiveness when he condemns you to hell"

"Save your speech for God" he spat.

"Oh, I will. I guarantee you I will. And after I'm done, there will be a place reserved for me in heaven. And you will watch me tower over you whilst you burn in the pits of the underworld. And the pain you feel won't come from the fire scorching your skin, it will come from watching women enter heaven too. It will hurt you to finally see a woman on a pedestal above you because your selfish, disgusting heart won't be able to take it. You may kill me, but you won't kill the idea. Long live Pariah's"

"Take him!" he screamed. "Take him before I kill him now!".

I smiled as they dragged me out of the tent for the last time.

A few days later, as the sun set, news spread of a baby girl that was born. Normally, she would've been sent to the Pariah zone, but there was no longer a zone to be sent to. Makni Armis no longer took any chances, and they found one small mark on her little skin and decided she would be better off in the ground.

The term honour killing was born.

We changed history, and in trying to better our futures, we made everyone else's worse. And here I was rotting in a Naghaar cell. Waiting for a miraculous day that I could somehow see freedom again. I wished I could hold her again. For one last time. I wanted to hold her for eternity, until the stars exploded and swallowed the earth whole. I wanted to hold her until every flower on earth died and every grain of soil dried up. I wanted to hold her for every second…every minute…. for every beat of my heart until my time ran out. But I couldn't because prisoners have the freedom to dream but not the freedom to live their dreams.

I didn't regret a single thing.

"Mum..." I whispered as the sunlight beamed through the iron bars. "I don't want you to feel as if you failed. I know this is not what you wanted for me, but you did everything right. You raised me with so much love, so much kindness that every single coin in the world could not repay a fraction of your sacrifices. Tell my baby brother that I look forward to playing with him and tell him that I will not cage him the way I did Meira. I'm sorry I couldn't get revenge for you. I'm sorry I couldn't hurt the men that took you away from me. Please forgive me"

Tears started flowing down my cheeks.

"It's true when they say the end of life gives you new perspective..."

Within the time it took me to relive my memories, the screech of the lock pulled me out of my senses. The walk wasn't long, as I dragged my feet and stepped out into the light a huge crowd had already gathered. They looked at me with scowling faces and pride seeping through their veins. In front of me was a large oak stump, and beside it a sharp axe that shone in the light. It had been newly sharpened. I couldn't tell you how I felt, because there was nothing left to feel. Second by second, I took my place in front of the stump, and they pushed my head down onto the warm wood. I closed my eyes, not wanting my last memory to be of the people of Naghaar.

I envisioned her beautiful silhouette dancing in the rain the first time we sat under the willow tree. I imagined the first time I touched her skin and how it created wildfires in the pit of my belly. And I imagined what could've been our future if I married her. If I could've been the father to her children and a husband to my wife. In the distance, the clouds began to darken, and the air suddenly turned cold. Within a few moments, droplets of rain began to fall onto my cheek, and it was at that moment I knew, she was somehow there with me.

But it all ended when the sound of the axe screeched, and my world went black.

The willow tree

Talia

I watched the trees sway gently in the wind as if they were all in a synchronised ballet performance. Each branch, jagged or smooth, short, or long, was wrapped up in a cocoon of beautiful colours. A single woodpecker was sat on the highest perch it could find. Its body was a stunning concoction of black and white but most noticeably was its nape, which was adorned in the most vibrant ribbon of crimson. The season of autumn had always been my favourite, but the season was disappearing now, and winter loomed around the corner. The colours on God's green earth made me feel as if I was living in a watercolour painting and I was the muse. But this world was far from a dream.

Every day since, I cried in a way I had never done before. It was the only way I could connect to every heartstring that orchestrated this body. It had been 5 months since I last saw Kalei. I had no idea if he was still alive. Meira had aged. She wasn't old and grey, but she reminisced about her brother as if she lived a million lifetimes with him. Since that day, we had been on the run with Jodie and the girls. But that day was different from the rest, because I wasn't running.

I stood at the edge of cliff. Meira had begged me, pleaded, cried, and wailed for me not to jump. I remember looking at her blank face, my deep sorrowful eyes stared back. I was detached from my body, soul, and mind. I told her that I had no purpose in this life. I said I could predict my life. Everywhere I would go everyone would see my forehead, and that anytime I would ever smile, the world would shun me as if I was a cursed woman. I told her how I would never find love, not after Kalei and if I ever was lucky enough, it would be for my body and not my face. If

I was ever lucky to be a mother to a child, that child would see a monster not a mother. No woman that looked like me survived in the world, and that a woman with imperfect skin could never life a perfect life. She asked me why I wanted to do this.

"Nothing will ever be the same" I cried. "I've waited months and all I see is the same greenery, hear the same whispers in the wind and the same isolated willow tree". And this was how I could end the pain, to somehow restore the balance in nature, by giving my life in return for the hope that Kalei's would return. Because he was worth more than one soul, he was my whole universe.

She cried and pleaded, and she desperately tried to convince me that things would get better. I apologised, said how sorry I was that because of me she lost her only family.

"You're my family now Talia!" she screamed. "DON'T YOU DARE LEAVE ME TOO!"

I turned to watch the paleness flood her face, her lips drain of colour and her eyes turn a blood red. She was on the brink of exploding. Losing all sense and direction. I took three long, large breaths and realised that I was the most selfish person in the world. I took a few steps back, until there was a bit of distance between me and the edge of the cliff. How could I abandon her when she needed me the most? How could I let Meira suffer in this world all alone? How would I be doing any justice for Kalei by leaving behind the one person he tried so hard to protect? I walked to her, placed my forehead on hers and stared deeply in her eyes. The same brown intensity that Kalei had, was also sifted in beautiful sprinkles in her iris. Although, he wasn't here, there was a part of him in her. And that meant I would need to hold onto her as if she were him. She held me tight, cried into my shoulder and thanked me a thousand times that I didn't jump. I held her too, but with no conviction. Saying to someone that you want to leave the world and thinking it are completely different things. She didn't know that I was falling apart inside. That every seam and fibre of my being had been dismantled and shredded. She didn't know that even now, every Sunday at 6am, I went back to the willow tree and sat under it in the hope that I would see him again.

I could've just ended my life and left this world. Why did everything go wrong? I lost Kalei, I lost Sami, I lost my home, I lost Zafinah. I lost everything that held together my dreams and the one group of women I never wanted to be a part of, the group of women I so badly wanted to escape, were the ones who saved me. Zafinah…if only I could tell her now how much I understood what belonging meant. But, whilst my world was ripping apart at the seams, I couldn't leave this world, because the truth was, yes, there was a pain associated to this world, but it was the only world I wanted to know, because he was once in it.

And just as my thoughts began to drift, the first drop of rain fell and as if almost by heart, I closed my eyes and began to twirl in the rain. I was afraid, afraid of the future and what it held for me. But for now, this moment had become a memory, one that I would cherish for the rest of my life. This was how it was supposed to feel like…having fallen in love. That even if the world was black and white, we were once the essence of colour in it.

But for now…I'll wait for you Kalei until my last breath…

Printed in Great Britain
by Amazon